LAYBACK

Cover Design by Graphics by Stacy
Formatting by Alyssa Garcia
Editing by Stephanie Atienza

For more information about Jennifer Rebecca & her books, visit:
www.jenniferrebeccaauthor.com

LAYBACK

USA TODAY BESTSELLING AUTHOR

JENNIFER
REBECCA

ABOUT THE BOOK

Not too long ago, I had one goal: Win an Olympic Gold Medal but an injury took me out of the running for the Ladies Figure Skating competition at the last Olympic Games. Nancy Kerrigan was grandfathered in. I was not.

Translation: I was disqualified. *DQ'd.* I was out in the cold on my keister.

But when an offer to fill a spot on a pairs team lands in my lap, I take it. It seems like an answered prayer—that is until a competitor is found brutally murdered in her room at the competitor's village and my partner is the number one suspect.

I'm going to have to take matters into my own hands. *Again.* Sweet Kristi Yamaguchi, save me from overly cocky men.

My name is Sophia Eleonore Dubois and holy mother of Dorothy Hamill my life is still complicated . . .

For Sean,

Because sometimes I have to take a minute and just be thankful, be in awe, of how very lucky I am. I don't know what I did in life to have the kind of karma that brought a man like you into my life but whatever it is, thank God that I did. You have blessed the kids and I in ways that I could never put to words with your love and dedication to us.

Thank you for being you.

And Also For Andrea,

Who shipped Kane and Sophia so hard she said "Thank hell you're writing another Sophie book" when I asked her for help. She's wildly talented and has the biggest heart and I'm so grateful for her friendship.

Layback:

This upright spin involves the skater leaning back at the head and shoulders. The classic layback spin features one leg being lifted up behind the skater and the arms extended out and upward. There are several variations on this spin, including the skater leaning toward the side rather than the back (sideways-leaning spin) or reaching back and grabbing the lifted skate (catch-foot layback spin).

www.sportslingo.com

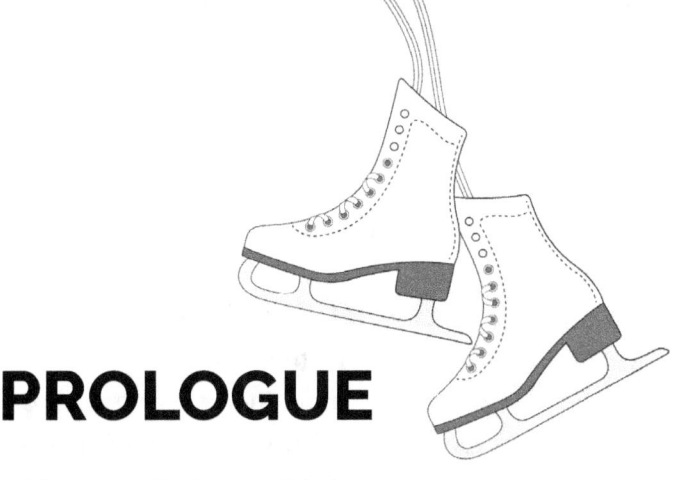

PROLOGUE

It's not what you think

"**S**weet Kristi Yamaguchi's daisy dress," I whisper more to myself than anyone else. "You have got to be kidding me."

"This is not what you think," Luc says and there is a note of panic in his voice that makes me back up a step.

"Really?" I ask as my anger rises to the surface. What kind of bubble headed moron does he think I am? I wasn't born yesterday. "Because it looks to me like you are standing over the dead body of our competitor."

"Okay," Luc says hesitantly. "It is what it looks like."

"Darn it, Luc!" I snap. "How could you?"

"What?" he says surprised. "You can't possibly think that I did this?"

"Well, I don't really know what to think right now, now do I?" I bite back.

"Sophie, please," he pleads. "You've got to believe me."

"This looks bad, Luc," I tell him. "Really, really bad."

"I know." He lets out a frustrated sigh and pushes a hand through his thick hair.

Luc and I stand there, facing each other with Layla's body sprawled over a chair between us. I'm not sure which is more disconcerting, the ropes tied around her nude body or the ones tied around her neck.

"Please don't run from me. I'm not going to hurt you."

"I'm not going to lie, Luc, this scares me," I admit.

"I know. Me too."

He sighs again and pulls his hand through his hair. The silence between us speaks volumes. This was supposed to be my second chance at the Games. My last one as a singles competitor was taken from me by my step-monster and her evil henchman when they broke my leg. So, when the opportunity to replace half of a pairs team came up, I jumped on it. Now, it seems like I should have paid more attention to the fine print.

"You have to believe me," he pleads with those big, brown puppy dog eyes that have probably gotten him out of more scrapes than he deserves.

I let out a sigh and admit, "I do."

"Thank fuck," Luc blurts out. "But what are we going to do now?"

I wish like heck that I knew myself. This is more

than a little complication.

"I don't know." What I do know is that my mostly on-again boyfriend, former professional hockey player and current San Diego PD homicide detective, Kane Fucking Green, is not going to be thrilled when he hears about this.

Kane is going to be so mad—he's going to be pissed—*excuse my French*.

My name is Sophia Eleanore Dubois, daughter of a United States Senator, still an Olympic hopeful figure skater, and holy mother of Dorothy Hamill, my life is still complicated . . .

ONE

Love triangles and trainings

I feel the weight of my skate bag on my shoulder as I pull open the door to my home rink, the *Del Mar Ice House*. The cool air hits my face and I feel a sense of calm invade my body as I breathe it in.

I've been back here more than once since my friend, Vadim, was killed but it never stops being fresh in my mind. No matter how much time has passed I still see his lifeless body spinning around the rink on his trusty Zamboni, his sightless eyes pointed at the Championship banners that hang from the ceiling before I see what is really before me.

The wound is still raw.

Vadim owned this rink until my stepmonster had him killed when he found out about her plans to have me kidnapped and sold overseas. Growing up, I had no idea that the woman who had married my father after my mom had died was a Russian sleeper agent. She had spent years making my life miserable to the point that I hid at the ice rink as much as I could. It became my home away from home and the only place where I could really be me—or as much as I could be me anywhere. The life as the daughter of a United States Senator is lived in the public eye. You have to watch your every move closely because the media is watching you even closer just waiting for you to falter.

My step-mother was no different. She held me to incredibly high standards. To her I was never smart enough, pretty enough, or thin enough. *And I thought competitive figure skating could be tough!* But to her, I was a representative of the Dubois family, and one that was sorely lacking. And somehow, through it all, I managed to find confidence on the ice where I could express myself in moves on the ice.

That is until a year and a half ago, my father and step-mother had positioned Kane-unbeknownst to me—as a Secret Service agent on loan from his day job with the San Diego PD assigned to me in Paris while my Precision Skating Team of six year olds competed in the World Championship. He was tasked to pose as a romantic hopeful in order to get close to me, and sadly, he was just a little too good at his job.

As my friend Shelby likes to say, I caught the feelings. Which would have been fine until I found out that it was just their way of keeping me out of trouble until they could scoop me up and hand deliver me to a grass roots Congressman that they were hoping to align themselves with for their own political gain and not, say, the happiness of their only daughter.

Silly me for thinking one was more important than the other.

My stepmonster had promised me to a Junior Congressman from San Diego. They had all secretly plotted to run with my dad in his bid for the White House on a family values platform with me as his wife. What a perfectly pretty little picture we would have made with my father and step-mother in the white house and my husband as second in command. And they could have fooled the whole country if only I was willing to fall in line.

And if that wasn't laughable enough considering he was also a Russian Sleeper Agent like my step-mother. When I didn't comply, they decided I could be sold to the highest bidder and shipped off to Eastern Europe never to be seen or heard from again.

But what had happened in Paris with Kane had broken me into a thousand little pieces. Like shards of glass, I didn't think that there was a hope in the world to put me back together again. Fortunately, it gave me the courage to finally stand up to my parents inreguards to what I was and was not willing to accept in terms of my life. Too bad that when I finally tried to take control of my own life, my step-mother had decided that I was no longer valuable. I had become a liability. So instead of gift wrapping me and handing me over on a silver platter to the handy dandy Congressman, she had decided to sell me to the highest bidder overseas. As it turned out, dear, old step-mommy had a side business in human traficking. Fun times, right?

I still struggle every day with the reality that the woman my father had trusted to raise me after my mother died was secretly plotting to sell me to the highest bidder and when that didn't work out she was going to let her partner who had become obsessed with me torture me for denying him. To make matters worse, my father and I have not rebuilt our relationship.

At the time I was training to fight for Olympic Gold in ladies figure skating. Who knows how it would have turned out? Maybe I would have choked like all the times before. I just don't know. But that time had felt different. I felt good. I felt ready.

And then it was all taken away.

I had done my best to stay away from them while I pursued my dreams. Keeping my nose out of their political machinations seemed like my best bet. Or so I had thought. Unfortunately, all of my dreams came crashing to the ground when I was punished for my indifference with a crowbar to the thigh.

My femur didn't just break, it shattered in two places and every hope I had for the Gold Medal went right out the window. I could have pushed my recovery and made it to the Games if I was grandfathered into the National Championship like Nancy Kerrigan was when she took her crowbar to the leg. Apparently, when you are the daughter of a sitting U. S. Senator, the Skating Union officials worry about looking like they are playing favorites. In fact, they worried so much that they didn't help me at all.

They didn't even send me a get-well card. *Or flowers for that matter.*

I'm not going to lie, that stung a little bit. But the worst part was I was out in the cold on my keister. That was my last chance—or so I had thought.

I still went through all the surgeries and rehab like a good girl even though on a good day I had thought my physical therapist was a sadist. I trained and was back on the ice with the synchronized figure skating team of little girls that I coached before I knew it. They were happy to have me back and I was glad to be there. My girls probably saved my life. They needed me and after my fall from grace it felt darn good to be needed.

It felt so great to be back on the ice even if it was just as a coach. In the mornings, I still got up early to hit the ice to practice footwork, moves in the field, jumps and spins. Not to mention, I choreographed a whole new set of routines for my sassy, little ladies.

We have a National Title to defend, after all.

When I was lucky, and Kane didn't have to be into the station too early, he would join me on the ice, encouraging me from close by. Truth be told, I'm not sure that I would have made it back to my top shape without him. I guess hockey players are tougher than they look. It was as close to perfect as I was ever going to get, and I was working my booty off to let go of what wasn't meant to be. My final chance at Olypmic Gold had slipped through my fingers when I took a crowbar to the leg and that's okay. I am alive—and dear, old step-mommy is now my dead, old step-mommy—and that is all that matters.

That is until I got the call.

One Wednesday afternoon, I was minding my own business and picking up my condo. Kane and I live next door to each other in the same luxury high rise downtown. On Wednesdays I run my laundry and change the sheets on my bed. I like to crank up some classic Britney Spears and get my Marie Kondo on.

I was halfway through ...Baby One More Time when my phone rang.

"Hello?" I had answered after sliding my finger across the bottom of the screen to unlock my phone.

"How you skate pairs?" my coach, Eugen—pronounced you-GIN—spoke in heavily accented English.

"What?" I had asked for clarification. Eugen is from the old country as he likes to put it. Really, he came to America sometime between Stalin and Putin and that's all that I have been able to confirm. Everything else he keeps tightly to the vest. After my step-monster's betrayal had cut so deep I was leery of everyone with any ties to Russia but Eugen. He was a harsh taskmaster before and even more so afterwards. I would always count on him to hit me in the back with a broken hockey stick for poor posture. And I needed that kind of consistency to move forward.

"Listen, girl!" he shouted in his accented voice which was really saying something because Eugen was pretty darn unflappable. I had never seen him raise more than an eyebrow, so this show of excitement was highly irregular. "I say 'how you skate pairs?'"

"Pairs?" I asked. "Like a man and a woman skating at the same time?"

"Da!" he said switching back to Russian. Honestly, with him this animated it probably was better to switch to a language that he was more fluent in. "Pairs!"

"I don't think I have ever competed in pairs," I had answered his previous question switching my answers to Russian. "Precision and singles, but never pairs."

"You learn fast," he had said, and I still wasn't able to keep up with the tennis match that was the conversation. When I switched to speaking Russian, Eugen switched to English and vice versa. He was going to give me whiplash.

"Thank you . . . I think." I still wasn't entirely sure what the nature of this phone call was about. Something about pairs and me but Eugen still hadn't calmed down enough to give me the meat and potatoes of it.

"You try out start Monday," he said switching back to English again. I'm good but even I am not that good! I was beginning to think that I may never get to the bottom of things with him.

"What tryout?" I asked.

"For Miller and Saucier," Eugen answered.

"Why would I tryout with them?" I had asked. "They are already a team." Not to mention an Olympic qualifying team. Must be nice, I had thought ungraciously. I let out an aggravated breath and cross my fingers that Eugen doesn't hear it over the line. I gave it my best effort to push down the jealousy that surged whenever I think about missing my last chance.

"Because Miller is pregnant, and they don't want anyone to know." I like when Eugen drops bombs and then decides to be totally calm. After all of his excitement, that was the last thing I had thought he would say.

"Holy triple axel, batman," I had mumbled. That was big. Like really, really big. Figure skaters needed squeaky clean images and an accidental pregnancy wouldn't help that along. It was already bad enough that her partner, Luc Saucier, was known for being kind of a man-whore.

"You can say that again," Eugen said switching back to Russian as his excitement mounts again.

"But what does that have to do with me?" I had asked.

"Saucier is Canadian," he answered.

"I know that," I said still not getting the point.

"Miller and Saucier qualified for the U. S. team but he is not American. He need U. S. skater for partner," he explained in English.

"Okay . . ." I hedged.

"That partner you."

With those words, Eugen had once again changed the course of my life. Just when I had thought that I was down and out, that there would be no more chances, one fell right in my lap. I knew, without a doubt, that I would grab hold of this opportunity and not let go. So, a few days later I covertly flew to Chicago to tryout with Luc Saucier to replace his pregnant partner.

Shortly after, Luc temporarily relocated to San Diego to train with me and my coach, Eugen, who is one of the best. And maybe to get a few digs in with Kane. I didn't know it at the time, but Luc was a professional hockey player before switching to pairs. He and his partner were a regular real life Cutting Edge.

I didn't know it until I returned home and caught up with my friends as Daisy and her friend, Alyssa were moving into a condo in the same development as Shelby. Apparently, I had missed all of the excitement as the gang rescued Alyssa and Shelby from a crazy man who was killing hookers—not that Shelby was a hooker but there was something I was missing about her pretending to be a hooker. Or whatever that means.

We had all laughed and joked as we helped them move their stuff into the new place, but it was over pizza when they had asked me how things had gone in Chicago that things took a decided turn when I had mentioned my new partner.

Kane had demanded that I not skate with Luc and I immediately saw red. I am not ever going to be with someone who controls my life again. The last time I let someone dictate my life had almost gotten me killed. And Kane knew that not to mention he has no right to demand that I sacrifice my dreams for his wounded pride.

So, I left without any pizza—which was the true crime—and I haven't talked to Kane since which has been difficult to pull off seeing as we live next door to each other and have the same set of friends. I have made myself perfectly clear. When he's ready to not be a huge jackass I will be willing to hear him out but not until then. I have come too close to finally realizing my goal and I'm not giving it up for anyone, least of all a man who demands that I do so for the sake of his over inflated ego. If Kane really cares for me, and I believe that he does, he will come around—eventually.

So here I am, stepping into the rink that I have always trained at for as far back as I can remember. This is the same place that my mom had taken me to for tiny tot classes so long ago, before she was taken from me and everything else fell apart. Before my dad was so lost in his own political machinatchions that he lost sight of protecting his only child.

So much has changed and yet, in some ways, it's

still the same. I still see Vadim, not in his glory as a renowned hockey coach, but struck down in his prime in the place that was his sanctuary above all else. That was a big part of what he and I had had in common. We were cut from the same cloth in many ways and this rink gave us the home that we needed. Vadim wasn't a hero, but in the end, he was mine. He had sacrificed his own life to protect me and for that, I will be weternally grateful. So I close my eyes and kiss my fingertips before touching them to the barrier glass around the ice and whisper a soft, "Thank you," into the air.

I take in a deep breath before stepping further into the bowels of my home away from home. A year ago, I would have cringed in frustration at Kane showing up to raid my practice time. Now, a part of me wishes he was here. I would be lying to myself if I said that I didn't miss him, and I really do. I miss his laughter and lines that crinkle around the sides of his eyes when he does. I miss the way that he makes me laugh and how that warmth travels through my body when I do. I miss the way that he made me feel safe and protected in a world that is anything but safe—a lesson that I learned the hard way not too long ago. I miss the confidence he had in me and the way that he looks at me like I can do absolutely anything in the world.

The sleepless nights are the worst. It's in those moments between awake and asleep that I rollover to reach for him to find nothing but an unslept in side of the bed and sheets that are cool to the touch are all hallmarks of the Kane sized hole he left in my life when he gave me an ultimatum that I couldn't cave into before I walked away. He had asked me to give up this chance, this last chance, at Olypmic sized redepmtion with Luc. For as long as I can remember, my only goal was to win an Olympic Gold Medal. Kane has one so he doesn't understand. Sure, his career was cut short by an elbow injury that sometimes still pains him, but he has already tasted the sweetness of victory that I have been continuously denied.

And when it was finally within my grasp after letting go of the one dream that I have held onto, I just could not do it, I couldn't give it up once and for all when it was my choice this time, not someone else's. So when Kane forbade me from skating with Luc, I lost my temper. I had channelled my dear friends, the Dangerous Dames, and in a rare show of pique, told Kane where he could stick his 1950's ideologies and walked out of the door and his life.

For a while or for good, I don't know. I just know that for now I have to live my life as if he's not coming back and that thought burns deep in my chest every time I let it take root. I can't help but wonder if I had made the correct decision.

But deep in my heart of hearts, I know that I cannot give in to what he wants me to do. To walk away from the dreams that I have spent my entire twenty-four years of life dreaming is something that I can't live with. My mother, God rest her soul, would be furious if she knew that I gave up everything, that I had changed everything, for a man who would not change for me.

She loved my father with everything she had, and it was that love that left her a target for a murderous sleeper agent. Her death left me living those consequences with a father who knew how to run a successful political campaign but didn't know how to parent a daughter and a stepmother who was more monster than mother.

I feel like I have the weight of the world on my shoulders as I step into the team box and drop my skate bag down to the rubber mats that line the floor. The air from my lungs bursts out of my mouth as I flop onto the bench leaning forward as I go to unzip my bag and pull out my skates.

I slip my chucks from my feet one by one and drop them into the bag followed by the rubber guards that protect my blades. I slip my feet into the soft but hard leather boots and wrap the laces around the hooks like I have always done before. At this point it's second nature and my mind wanders without my permission. Sadness flows through my veins when I picture Kane and his megawatt smile. I miss him. I know that I do, but until he understands where I'm coming from we don't have anything to talk about. I know that walking away when I did was the right thing to do. So, I do what I can—for now—and grab my water bottle and my MP3 player setting both on the low wall of the team box and zip my bag closed.

I stretch my arms up over my head and lace my fingers together as I push up through the stretch. I pull in a deep breath and slowly lower my arms, rolling my shoulders back into a perfect ballet stance that only years of classical training could instill. Carefully, I extend my leg to raise it up and place my heel on top of the low wall as if it were a ballet barre and lean into the stretch, raising my arm slowly up overhead.

I turn on my standing foot so that my hips are facing forward and deliberately drop forward inch by measured inch until my nose touches my knee. I let out even breaths as I count to ten before pulling myself to stand back up straight again.

I pivot on my standing foot one last time so that I am standing with my free leg stretched out behind me on the wall and slowly walk my hands down the wall until they rest flat on the rubber mats of the ground and lean into the stretch. I feel tingle run up the back of my neck like someone is watching me—but that can't be. I know that I am the only one in the rink this early in the morning. Besides, this is my day to practice on my own and work on choreography.

I was lucky that Eugen and Luc's coach both agreed that my choreography skills are Olympic worthy and gave me the chance to work with them on our programs for the games. It's an honor to be trusted with such a huge responsibility, but the weight of that responsibility sits heavily on my shoulders.

I pull in a deep breath and the push it out purposefully before standing back up and lowering my leg to the ground. I switch legs to repeat my movements on the other side. The process not only warms up my muscles before a heavy workout but also clears my mind of everything that I can't do anything about right now.

I push open the gate from the team box and step down onto the ice. I cue up my warm up music and shake my arms out as I take a couple of steps out before pushing out to warm up. I take a couple of laps, leaning into each stroke before I turn around and move into a salchow. I push myself through all of my jumps starting first with singles and then moving into a series of doubles before working my way up to triples. With Luc, timing will be everything, so I need to be at my best when skating with him. The last thing I want to do is be a weak partner to him when this is likely my last chance at the Games. I won't choke. This time, everyone will be proud.

I cue up the music for our short program. I had the idea that since people are already talking about us what with Luc's old partner quietly exiting stage left and me taking her spot for the biggest competition ever that we should at least have a little fun. I thought a Bonnie and Clyde theme for both the short and the long programs would do the trick and surprisingly, Luc and our coaches agreed.

We have been practicing this routine for a few months now. For the amount of time we have had I think we're doing pretty good, but only a clean skate the day of and the judges will determine how we rank.

I run through the programs several times before deciding that I feel pretty good about my ability to perform them with Luc. I have a few more minutes left of my time slot and like I always do when I am alone, I run through my old program. The one that I would have skated in the National Championship if I hadn't been disqualified when my leg was broken.

The one that I was sure I would have won with.

This program was my last chance to go it alone, to finally prove that I could do it. Not choke and place fifth at the games. This was the program that I was sure would bring me the gold and now I just can't seem to let go of it.

Sure, there will be more Games after this one, but not for me. After the attack that left my femur shattered in places, my body, even at only twenty-three is done. I don't have another four-year cycle in me. Truth be told, I didn't before the attack either. I knew I was done then just as much as I am now.

I'm just rounding the back of the rink and as I glide across the diagonal, I lean back into a deep Bauer. The tip of my ponytail skims the ice and I close my eyes and just let myself feel like I'm flying.

That is until I hit the boards.

But I don't really hit the boards. What I hit was a muscle bound, oversized man. A man that smells overly familiar. This man is Kane Fucking Green and I'm not speaking to him. I feel my body stiffen and I try and get away from him but his arms band tighter around me.

"Let me go," I demand.

"No," he growls out. "You are going to fucking talk to me."

"I am not."

"Yes, you are."

I shake my head like a stubborn child. "No, I'm not and you can't make me."

"Watch me," Kane says before he scoops me up over his shoulder and carries me off the ice. Without breaking stride he snags my skate bag, which I notice has already been packed up, and carries us both out the door.

Kane tosses my skate bag into the bed of his truck without a care before pulling open the passenger door of his old blue Tacoma. He drops me on my backside in the seat before slamming the door closed. I sit and stare at my skates still on my feet as they sit against the worn mats on the floorboards. I notice Kane doesn't have skates on his feet as he runs around the truck. He must have jogged out to grab me in his running shoes and that's not easy to do. Part of me wants to be impressed but the other part is just mad that he seems to be kidnapping me. I get kidnapped a lot lately and that kind of chafes a bit.

He pulls open the driver's door and jumps in. He fires up the truck and peels out.

"What about my car?" I shout as I try and buckle

my seatbelt.

"I'm having a rookie drive it home," that's all he says to me by way of explanation. Nothing more, like why he's taken me or where we are going.

And to be totally honest with myself, I don't want to know. I can't even bother to care because for the first time in months, I am breathing in the same air as Kane and it is suddenly sweeter.

TWO

I'm not speaking to you

I n the short amount of time that I have been in this vehicle with Kane Fucking Green, I have decided that he is nothing short of a menace.

No, he's an overgrown ape of a man who is too used to getting his own way. Well, I have news for him! I can be every bit of the ice princess he had once accused me of being. I have a lifetime of practice under my belt as not only the daughter of a popular politician, but also as a competitive athlete on the toughest stage. If he wants a display of stubborness and posturing, I will be happy to give him one.

I fold my arms across my chest and press my lips together in a tight line in order to express my displeasure at his barbaric behavior and I lean back in my seat. I refuse to say another word to Kane for the remainder of this ridiculous drive to who knows where.

Kane, obviously wise to my plans, lets out a heavy

sigh. "Fine," he says. "Be that way."

"Oh, I will be any way that I darn well please," I mumble under my breath. Unfortunately for me, Kane has the hearing of a bat and smirks.

"You do remember how turned on it makes me when you go all ice princess, don't you?" he asks and I shoot a quick glance at the sizeable bulge in the front of his jeans. The sight makes my mouth go a little dry and I'm not going to lie, I miss that too.

I open my mouth to tell him just exactly how turned on I can make him and what I would do about it when I remember that I am not supposed to be speaking to him. Out of the corner of my eye I see his arrogant smirk as I snap my jaw closed.

Heaven save me from overly cocky men.

Kane thinks he knows everything about me. He thinks I will eventually capitulate to his demands because he's got a spectacular body and he knows what to do with it. Well, he's got another thing coming to him if he thinks I'll cave to his wishes just because he can make my own body sing.

I pout—and that's exactly what I did, I pouted like a spoiled child—but what else was I supposed to do for the remainder of this drive.

I was so lost to my own sulking that I didn't realize we had arrived at the exclusive high rise at the beach that caters to the upper echelon of San Diego County, a place where both Kane and I own luxury condos, until he pulled his truck into the underground garage. Well, hell.

Honey, we're home . . .

"Stay," he barks at me when he kills the engine before climbing from the truck and rounding the hood. His terse command does nothing but stoke the flames of my own anger and I feel my face burn in humiliation at being scolded like a puppy who peed on the carpet. I didn't extricate myself from under the abusive thumb of my Russian spy step-mother only to fall into the command of a bossy man. *No, thank you.*

Before I can even move, Kane is swinging open the passenger door and reaching across me to unbuckle my seatbelt. He scoops me up and over his shoulder—*again*—like a sack of flour and I want to argue that I can walk on my own but then I realize that I am still wearing my skates and can't walk on concrete in them.

"Do you have to carry me like that?" I snap.

"Do you have to act like a spoiled brat?" Kane barks back as he punches the call button for the elevator and I feel the heat of my embarrassment burn up my neck and across my face, further than before. I did act like a spoiled brat and I shouldn't have but there is something about this man that brings out the worst in me. But also, if I'm being honest with myself, he also has the ability to bring out the best. "Well?" he asks as he lands a hard swat on my backside.

"Hey!" I shout. "What was that for?"

"Are you going to answer me?" he snaps as the doors open and he pushes the button for our floor.

"I don't even know what the question was any-more," I grumble as I try and reach behind me to rub the sting out. Kane brushes my hand away and I let it fall back down behind him.

"I asked if you were going to keep being a brat?" he says as he caresses the spot where he inflicted pain as he steps off the elevator and prowls down the hall to where we both live—next-door to each other.

"No," I mumble mostly to myself as he unlocks his front door and lets us inside. "But you don't have to be such a brute either."

"That's true enough," Kane says on a sigh as he lets me slide down his body to land sitting on the marble topped island in his kitchen. "It seems where you are concerned I just can't help myself."

"That is kind of unfortunate," I mumble mostly to myself than the room at large as Kane slides his strong hands down my leg until he reaches my booted foot. Heat blooms in his wake and I shift in my seat as he expertly plucks the laces and pulls the skate from my foot.

"It can be," he says as he repeats his process down my other leg before removing my second skate. "I like to think it's because there's so much passion between us that we sometimes let it get away from us. But the key to that is not burning each other in the process."

And he is not wrong either.

"I can't help but feel a little singed at the moment," I admit and instantly want to recall the words—no matter how true they are—when I see the look of pain that flashes across Kane's handsome face for a split second before he softens his look at me and buries his own hurt feelings so that I can no longer see them play out over his chiseled features.

"I know, honey, and you have no idea how sorry I am for it," he tells me in a quiet voice.

"Try me," I tell him honestly. I don't want to hate Kane and truthfully, I don't. I just want to get through this last Games and then we can figure out where to go from there. But he can't bully me around either and he has to come to terms with that and how much it hurt me too.

"Saucier and I have a history," he begins to tell me his sordid tale.

"I kind of had a feeling that you did when you blew up on me in Alyssa and Daisy's apartment a few weeks ago."

And he did.

I had just returned home from a successful tryout with Luc and his coach feeling on top of the world and ready to hit the ground running as we trained. Luc and I had agreed to train here in San Diego to pull the attention away from his partner who would continue to live in Chicago. But when I had told Kane and our friends about my new windfall, Kane had become furious and forbade me from skating with Luc in front of everyone.

I had never been so humiliated, and I hadn't spoken to Kane since then, but it wasn't for lack of trying on his part. Kane had called me several times every day and when I wouldn't answer for him, he had resorted to pounding on my front door and demanding entry every night. But I couldn't let him in. Kane had to know that I wouldn't be treated like a wayward child anymore. I am now in the driver's seat of my own life. But a small voice in the back of my head admits that he won't know my feelings on the matter until I give them to him once and for all.

I can't help but wonder now if maybe I was too harsh in my decision not to hear him out. Maybe I wouldn't have had to spend the last six weeks feeling cold and alone if I had just explained to him why his harsh words had hurt me so badly. Maybe, just maybe, we could have put all of this behind us weeks ago.

"What happened?" I ask.

"He fucked my wife," Kane says softly.

I'd like to say I was a rational human being but there seems to be a siren blaring in my ears set off by Kane softly whispering that he has a wife. I never thought of myself as jealous before, but this unnamed female who married the man that I have been in love with for the better part of a year and a half has me wanting to hurl my breakfast all over the natural stone tile that makes up his kitchen floor.

"Your wife?" I practically shout.

"Yes." Kane nods his head solemnly while a bleak look steals over his face.

"You're married!" I'm shouting. I can hear the

shrill tone to my voice and yet, there is nothing I can seem to do about it. I am freaking out.

When Kane first pursued me over a year ago, he was still involved with a woman named Lacy. Perfect fucking Lacy who wanted nothing more than to be the perfect wife for Kane. I had overcome a lot of jealousy and hurt feelings where she was concerned—mostly because after Paris, I couldn't even think about dating anyone else and Kane had managed to find a fantiastic substitute to warm his bed in no time at all. Clearly, his feelings didn't run as deep for me as mine had for him after our sordid run in France.

But to hear that on top of all that he had a wife too, I feel like a pressure cooker that is about to blow.

Kane rolls his eyes. "Was," he explains. "And only for a hot minute. Did you miss the part where I said my teammate fucked her?"

"I'm still stuck on the part where there ever was a *her* to begin with," I gripe under my breath and Kane smirks making my mood darken even further.

"I like this jealous side of you," he rumbles in that deep way that lets me know he's turned on. I, however, do not find it amusing at all.

"I am not jealous," I pout.

"You so are," he says on a laugh. "And I love it."

"Well, I'm not sure I find this situation so amusing," I admit petulatnly.

Kane leans in and softly brushes his lips against mine. "I do," he whispers against my mouth before pressing deep to push his tongue between my lips. I get lost in the moment, lost in Kane, in his spicy smell and the way that he surrounds me completely.

He pulls back to look me in the eye and I frown as I try to catch my breath.

"One, she's a total bitch and you have nothing to worry about," Kane explains. "Two, I was young, dumb with too much money in the bank, and had a hard on for the first pretty girl that smiled at me. Not to mention, you were like fourteen at the time."

I let out a frustrated sigh. "Still . . ."

"You're the only woman for me," he says softly as he presses his forehead to mine. "And I didn't treat you like I should have."

"It's okay," I say softly even though we both know that it's not. "I understand now." And really, I do. I would be furious if one of my friends had slept with Kane. I couldn't forgive it. It does give me new insight into Shelby and what a strong woman she really is. I probably would have killed her ex-fiance and her ex-bestfriend ages ago.

"It's not okay," Kane admits as he skates his nose down my cheek and tucks his face into the crook of my neck. "And I won't stand in your way anymore."

"Thank you," I say softly. The kisses that he is trailing down the side of my neck are starting to distract me but I hear his words and I appreciate them. I also understand what giving them to me is costing him as well.

"I understand how much these Games mean to you and I never should have said what I did," he says softly.

"No, you shouldn't have," I agree as he sucks on the tender skin behind my ear. "But it's in the past now."

"I'll be there cheering you on," he says before pulling my earlobe into his mouth and biting down on it.

"W-what are you doing?" I ask. My head is lost to the way that only Kane can make me feel.

"Making you some serious promises," he explains. In a serious tone but I can feel his broad smile against my neck.

"Oh, o-okay," I mumble as he cups my breast in his large palm over my clothes.

"And I'm going to be nice to Saucier," he promises as he circles his thumb around my nipple never letting it come in contact with the tip even though that is exactly what I want.

"Good." I arch trying to force hip to touch me where I want him to but Kane only lets out a rough chukle instead as he is wise to my manipulations and obviously enjoying watching me squirm

"And if he tries to see you naked I'm going to break his kneecaps," he rumbles next to my ear.

"Kane!" I shout but it ends on a moan as Kane finally gives me what I want with a little bit of bite as he pinches my nipple through the material of my clothes.

"What?" he says not sounding even a little bit sorry.

"He's not going to see me naked," I promise him.

"That's right, baby," Kane says as he glides his other palm up from my waist to cover my breast. He strokes my nipple through the velvet material of my practice dress. "I like this little green dress, honey."

"You do?" I ask breathlessly.

"Oh, yeah. With all of your honey blonde hair piled up on top of your head like that it makes you look just like Tinkerbell—*my Tinkerbell*," He growls just before biting down on the juncture of my neck and shoulder.

"Yes," I breathe as I tip my head to the side to give his mouth better access to my collar bone where he's layering an equal amount of nips and kisses.

"And you don't wear a bra under it," he explains further as he pinches my nipple again but this time even harder.

"W-what are you doing?" I ask him.

"Making it up to you," Kane says softly as he slides both his hands up behind my neck to unfasten the hooks of my dress. I shrug my shoulders out of the wide velvet straps of the soft material as he slides them down my arms, exposing my breasts, the tips illustrating exactly how much Kane affects me and he smiles a predatory smile at me that catches my breath in my throat.

Kane follows the wake of my dress with his mouth as he kisses his way down to one of my breasts and sucks the pink tip deep into his mouth. I feel the pull burn between my legs and spread them wider so that he can settle his sip between them. I rock against him, losing my self in the sparks that light up against my body as I press the neediest part of my body against his denim covered erection.

Kane lets my nipple go with a pop before backing away a bit to roll my dress down my legs bunching it in his large hands as he goes before dropping it to the kitchen floor so that I sit on the marble countertop in nothing but a pair of beige tights. I whimper at the loss of contact between his body and mine but fortunately, Kane doesn't make me wait long.

"I'm not sure there's anything to make up for," I say and even to my own ears, my husky voice is un-recognizable. I reach for him and pull the worn, gray hoodie and t-shirt underneath it up and over his head as one before gliding my palms over his muscular chest, the muscles bunching and twitching in my wake.

It would seem that I am not the only one affected here.

Kane slides his hands into the waistband of my tights and pulls them down exposing me to his heated stare. I wiggle to assist him as he slips the bits of sheer material from my body before dropping it to the floor with the rest of our discarded belongings.

As I sit nude on the cool stone countertop my body is on fire. A fire that is never fully extinguished, only banked until the next time Kane brings it scorching back to life.

"But baby?" Kane calls to me as he runs his palms up my naked thighs towards my center.

"Yeah?" I moan in response to his touch.

"Making up is the best part," he says before crushing his mouth to mine in a savage kiss and I have to admit that he's right. I wrap my arms around him and hold on tight.

I pant trying to catch my breath but it's no use when he breaks our kiss to watch me as he slides his hand to my center. I still clutch on to his shoulders as he runs his finger through my slit and seems to like what he finds there as he lets out a rough growl.

"Wet," he rumbles. "You're so damn wet for me, Tinkerbell."

"Yes," I pant as he slides just the very tip of his finger around my opening.

"Tell me it's only for me," he commands as he taps his finger against my clit making me squirm. "Tell me that I'm the one that makes you wet."

"Yes," I agree not because I will tell him anything that he wants to hear in this moment if only he will make me come, but also because it's true. There is no one for me but Kane Fucking Green and his magic fingers. "It's only you. It's all for you."

"Tell me that it's my cock that your pussy hungers for," he growls as he slides two fingers inside me and begins to pump them. His thumb replaces his finger on my clit and presses down as his finger find that spot deep inside me that has the ability to make me see stars. It's been so long since we've been together and my body burns so bright it won't take long to send me into bliss. And Kane knows it because he slows is fingers when I don't answer immediately. "Tell me."

"Yes, yes!" I practically yell as I buck my hips against his hand.

"Yes, what?" he asks. Kane knows that I hate to use dirty words, but he like to see me come undone completely and only for him.

"It's your c-cock that I hunger for," I admit, and he rolls his thumb over my clit but only once.

"What hungers for my cock?" he asks with a mischievous twinkle in his blue eyes but I haven't come this far only to be denied the climax that I want so badly.

"M-my pussy," I answer him.

"Good girl," Kane praises me as he pumps his fingers again, curling them so that they stroke that spot within me. "Do you know how hard it makes me to know that this good girl, so prim and proper, burns so hot for me?"

"No." I have to bite down on my bottom lip to keep from screaming as he continues to stroke me.

"And you do, don't you? You burn so hot for me?" he asks.

"Yes." He swirls his thumb again and I'm so close.

"Do you know how much I want you when I see how hot you are for me? For my cock?" he demands, and I need him so much. My fingers flex against his hard shoulders and my nails dig deep as he plays with me.

"Show me," I plead to him.

Kane slide his fingers free from my body and pushes my legs wide open. I drop down to lean on my elbows and watch him as he leans over me. My thighs tremble with anticipation as runs the blade of his nose along the side of my slit.

When he presses his thumb to my clit again, I whimper. But it's when he spears my center with his tongue that I scream my release as he licks me through it, making my arousal burns higher than before. Almost as if I hadn't come at all.

"Kane," I beg. "I need you."

"What do you need?" he smirks as he stands back up to tower over my body.

"I need you to fuck me." I can barely believe the words that leave my mouth but it's true. I need him so badly. Only Kane can put out the fire inside me that hurts so badly. "I need you inside me."

"And you'll have me," he says as he prowls up my body.

"I can't wait," I explain as I reach for him, plucking at the buttons that line the front of his jeans. I slide my hand inside and grip his hard length. "I can't wait," I repeat as I try and pull him towards me.

"Hold on, honey," he says as he pulls back. But I don't want him to pull back. I am desparate for him, to feel his hard length spear deep inside me.

"I can't wait," I shift trying to get him closer, but he denies me as he reaches into his back pocket and pulls out his wallet. Kane plucks a foil wrapper from inside and drops the folded leather to the floor before tearing it open with his teeth.

"I won't take your dreams from you, honey. We'll find them together," he says looking into my eyes as he rolls the latex down his impressive length. "Now, you can have me," he says before sliding all the way in on one thrust of his hips. He lets out a rough groan as he does.

"Kane," I call out as I wrap my legs around his hips and pull his shoulders to me. The result is me sitting up on the counter while he leans over me.

He holds me tight in his arms as he slides out slowly only to thrust back in. "I'm right here, Tink. I'm always right here," he growls as he pumps in and out of my body in a steady rythum. "This is right where I am meant to be."

Kane slides his length out only to slam back in once more, and then twice, before the tight grip he has on his control seems to break and he pounds into me faster and faster, harder and harder than before. The steady pace he had previously set is long since gone and I love it. This coupling is not soft and sweet, but rough and a little wild, *just like Kane*. After what we've been through the last month and a half, it's exactly what we need.

The fire in me burns hotter and hotter as Kane hurdles me towards another climax. I rake my nails down his back and whimper.

"That's it," he shouts as he pumps harder and harder. "Mark me. Make me yours."

"Kane—" I call out. It's too big and too fierce. I'm afraid it might break me when I let go. Or I might even be completely changed all over down to the very last molecule of me.

"Let go," Kane softly commands and I do, calling out his name as I fall. "Thank fuck," he says before he presses his face into the crook of my neck and growls as he follows me into bliss.

We lay like that for minutes, maybe hours, as we touch and kiss, just breathing each other in before he lifts me into his arms. This time not like a sack of flour but like a bride, like someone so precious that he never wants to let go of.

Kane carries me into his bedroom and lays me out in the middle of his huge bed. My hair is falling all around me, my bun long gone and I'm sure I look like a mess, but he looks at me like he's never seen anyone more beautiful before.

Somewhere along the way he tossed the condom from the kitchen and shimmied out of his jeans because I watch with rapt attention as he slides a new one down his impressive length. Kane prowls up the bed to cover my body with his. I spread my legs so that he can settle in between them and we lay like that without a care for the outside world, time means nothing as we touch and kiss each other with a gentle reverence.

By the time that Kane slide his fingers against my

center it is no surprise that I am ready for him. He rises up on his knees just enough so that he can slide his hard length through my wetness without losing the full contact between us once . . . twice . . . I let out a whimper when he glides against my clit a third time and thankfully, Kane decides to put me out of my misery.

Kane notches the tip of his cock to my opening and I gasp as he slowly pushes deep inside with one thrust. Everything is more sensitive after our fierce reunion in the kitchen but it only serves to make this time better because of it.

This time, Kane makes love to me. And it's soft and slow and gentle like the rolling waves of the ocean as he slips and slides in and out of my body. And even though this time is sweet and tender it is no less erotic.

My climax washes over me as Kane keeps his steady pace as he plunges in and out of my core with a loving ruthlessness and whisper his name as I come, "Kane."

Kane thrusts one more time before planting himself deep inside me and follows me over the edge, calling out my name not like a curse but like prayer as he does, "Sophia."

In the end, I was right, I am forever changed. We are no longer two lonely individuals but have been remade into two halves of the same whole.

And Kane was also right when he said we would accomplish our goals together. Because there is absolutely no way we could go on alone ever again.

THREE

The foregone foreskin conclusion

Buzz . . . buzz . . . buzzzzz . . .

My phone bounces around on the nightstand as it softly plays Britney Spears. *It's time to work, bitch.* And this morning I have a practice skate with Luc. We have been working so hard these past few weeks and things are finally coming together. I am so thankful for this opportunity that I don't want to let Luc and our coaches down so I try and get to the rink extra early so that I am warmed up and ready to go. I don't want any of them waiting on me.

I look back over my shoulder to where Kane is sleeping. His eyes are still closed, and his breaths come evenly. Good, he's still asleep and after last night's revelations, I don't want to wake him up. We are finally in a good place again and I'm not going to throw Luc in his face the very next day. I'm not going to be the one to rock the boat this time.

I gently lift the covers and cautiously slide out from underneath them. If I was focused on anything other than not waking Kane up, I would have noticed that he, and other parts of his anatomy, were very much awake long before his arm tightens around my waist and hauls me back into the bed.

"Eeek!" I squeal as he surprises me.

"Where are you going, Tink?" Kane rasps, his voice still husky with sleep and other things. "I don't know if I'm ready to let you leave this bed yet."

"Well, you don't have a choice because I have an early practice this morning," I inform him with a little softness in my voice so that he knows that I am not choosing the rink over him. "But I'll be back later."

Kane lets go of me and I slide out of bed and start pulling clothing that I had left here before we stopped speaking from drawers. I notice that Kane is flinging the covers back and pushing up from the bed to stand nude in all his morning glory—and I do mean *glory*—which I see prominently when he turns to the side before facing away again. His firm backside is turned towards me and I watch the muscles in his body play as he stretches out.

"Wh-what are you doing?" I ask before I give my brain a chance to catch up with my mouth. I should probably get some coffee in me before I sign my life away.

"Getting up," he says with a smirk playing about his mouth.

"I . . . uhh . . . I see that," I mumble as I stare at his erection. I can't help it. It's like there's a sexual tractor beam that draws my eyes directly to his long, hard cock.

"My eyes are up here, baby," he says with a chuckle and my eyes snap up to his. "I meant that I was getting out of bed to go with you."

"Oh . . ." Well, that's not at all embarassing. Kane has the ability to wipe all thought from my brain with a set of glutes that I know for a fact that I can bounce a quarter off of them because I have already tried.

I lose my train of thought as I watch Kane pull a pair of lighter wash jeans out of a drawer and slide them up his legs without underpants. They way that the smooth material molds to his muscular legs and . . . other assets shows how well-worn they are. Not to mention spending the day knowing that there is nothing standing in between my hand and what I so desperatly want but a few buttons and some well worn marterial is going to play havoc in my mind all morning. He pulls a white t-shirt over his head then grabs a gray hoodie and tosses it on the bed before grabbing a pair of socks and running shoes.

"Sophie?" he calls my name making me snap to attention.

"What?" I ask still distracted by the though of him going comando. I wonder if I would be able to tell if he was even a little bit hard because the material is so soft and plyable. If I was paying more attention to what

I was trying not to pay attention to I would definitley have my answer.

"You were staring . . ." he trails off in explanation.

"Huh?" I slow blink once . . . twice . . . three times to clear the fog from my brain but all I can see is Kane's huge . . . uhh . . .

"You're staring." He smirks. "And if you keep on staring at me like that Tink we're going to be about an hour late." That snaps me back into consciousness.

"No!" I shout as he prowls closer. "We don't have time."

"I'll be quick," he hums as he pushes me back onto the bed and somehow scooping up the shirt of his that I slept in last night and pulling it over my head to throw down to the floor like the practiced sex magician that he is—leaving me naked.

"How quick?" I ask before I can stop my mouth from asking what my brain knows that it shouldn't. I don't have time to play with Kane. I can't be late for practice.

"Fast," Kane says as he flicks open the buttons on those jeans that he wears all too well and lets his hard length spring free. He leans down over me. And I was going to be early anyways, now I'll just be on time. That's good enough. I can afford to be fast with Kane.

"Not *too* fast," I complain.

"No, baby. Not too fast," he says just before he crashes his mouth down on mine and slides deep inside me. Kane hits that spot that makes my eyes roll back in my head and all rational thought goes right out the window.

There are no words spoken as he moves in and out of my body while he presses his mouth to mine. I gasp as he hooks my knees around his elbows and drives in deeper and deeper as he thrust into my waiting pussy again and again. He sets a punishing rythum that promises to send us both over the edge sooner than later. Kane was clearly serious about his prose to go fast. I hold tight to his shoulders. It's all can do to keep me tethered to the earth the way that he has me spinning out of control with his magic cock.

Kane reaches between us and presses his thumb to the spot between my legs making them shake and I'm helpless to stop them. It's all that I need to send me over the edge and a scratch my nails down his chest scoring his skin as my orgasm crashes over me.

Kane pumps once, twice more before rising up to his knees pulling free from my body. He wraps his fist around himself and I can't help but watch as he strokes his hard cock. He looks so sexy with his jeans open just enough to expose himself. His ice blue eyes lock with mine as he rolls his bottom lip between his teeth. Kane lets out a rough groan as hot ropes land across the sheet between us as he comes.

And in the end, Kane was right. He could be fast but not *too* fast.

And we weren't late at all.

And wonders never cease to amaze . . .

"You okay, honey?" Kane asks from behind me as he grips my shoulders firmly in his hands.

"It's just—" I stop myself from finishing the thoughts that plague me every time I set foot in this rink. I don't want to feel this way every time I come here.

This is my home away from home, the place where I found comfort after my mom died, the place where I belonged when I no longer belonged at home with my father and stepmonster. The place I found solace to lick my wounds no matter where they came from.

"It's just what?" he asks in that rough voice of his.

I let out a sigh knowing that I am going to have to answer Kane. "It's just . . . different now. This place isn't the same since—" I swallow back against the tears that clog my throat when I think of my lost friend.

"Since Vadim was killed here," Kane finishes what I can't.

"Yeah."

We stand like that for a while, Kane behind me, lending me his strength. And I let him. I take it, self-ishly, because what I didn't realize while we were apart was how much I had not only missed but needed his quiet support.

This morning after Kane proved how fast he could be, we dressed as quickly as possible—Kane faster than me because he never really took off his jeans to begin with—it must be nice to be a man. I threw on black leggings over tights and a couple of tank tops layered over a sports bra. I pulled on a long-sleeved t-shirt and then a fleece zip up. I'll warm up once I really get moving on the ice and then shed some layers as I work up a sweat.

I slid my feet into a pair of pink Ugg boots with little bows on the back while Kane tied his running shoes. He tucked his wallet and badge into his pocket and a sidearm into the holster at the back of his jeans.

I'm not going to lie, it was hot watching it then and I'm a little warm thinking of it now. I never thought about guns other than the knowledge that the Secret Service Agents assigned to watch over my family were armed even though I never saw them. When my life was planned out for me, I was supposed to find a polite professional whose image could be used ruthlessly to further my father's political career. It was never expected that I would marry a police officer or a Federal Agent, both occupations which pad Kane's resume. And I can't help but think that maybe some day I might like to marry him. Of course it's way too soon to be day dreaming about those things so I brush off the thoughts and move on.

Then I picked up my skates where we left them in the kitchen before we left the condo and Kane locked the door behind us. We rode the elevator down to the parking garage where we climbed into his truck and he drove us down to my home rink in Del Mar.

But when we walked through the front door, all the events of the last year hit me like a ton of bricks, just like they always do and now here we are.

"We're going to get through this," his deep voice rumbles sending shivers up my spine and a warmth blossoms in my chest. In this moment, my mind is catching up with what my heart already knows . . .

Kane already holds my heart in the palm of his capable hands.

And then Luc ruins it when he skates by and bangs on the glass.

"Are you coming or what?" he asks with a smirk.

Oh no.

I feel the tension enter Kane's body and not leave. I have to do something to diffuse the situation—and fast. Unfortunately, I would find out later that it was the wrong choice.

"I'm coming!" I shout naively as I snatch up my skates where I dropped them by the door and head for the team box.

"Not yet," Luc calls out casually. "But give me a few minutes in a dark locker room and you will be."

"Luc," I say trying to stop him when I hear Kane let out and angry growl. Honestly, he sounds more lion than man right now. I'm equal parts turned on and alarmed. Who knew that his possessive caveman act would do things to me in unspeakable places? Certainly not me.

I kick my shoes off as I sit down on the bench as

fast as I can and slip my feet into my skates. I lace them up with quick and efficient moves. I've been doing it for so many years now that I could probably do it blindfolded so it doesn't take me long to lace them up.

I race through my stretches before pushing open the gate from the box and jumping onto the ice. I pass several laps around the rink to warm up both forward and backward before stopping back at the gate to take off my jacket.

"Ready to warm up with me?" I ask Luc.

"Baby, I'm already hot for you, but for you, I would be willing to do just about anything," he says before taking hold of my hand and pulling me into a basic hold so that we can warm up together.

I roll my eyes before moving around the rink with him. Luc is such a pain in my behind. I'd like to say that he's more trouble than he's worth, but I think under his man-ho ways is really man with a good heart. I have yet to prove it, but I'm sure it's there.

Mostly.

I'm pretty sure.

It has to be in there somewhere, right?

"Let's run some jump combos before Eugen gets here," Luc says to me.

"Okay," I agree, and we run our jump combos for both routines. Luc is a great jumper. He's really an amazing athlete in his peak physical fitness. If I wasn't madly . . . well, you know . . . with Kane and he wasn't worse than an alley cat, I would probably be attracted to him.

But alas, there is *only one* overly cocky man for me.

"Let us work on the lifts today!" Eugen shouts as he steps onto the ice. "To the lift HAR-ness!"

Luc and I skate over to the far end of the rink where Eugen is pulling a harness on a rope and pulley system over the glass topped wall. Because it is the backstage, short end to the rink the glass halves of the walls are lower here.

Luc holds me up while I step into the legs of the harness and tighten the buckles. It looks a lot like a rock-climbing harness handing on a giant coat hanger which is really a giant wooden triangle that keeps the harness upright on the rope and pulley system that runs over the short end of the ice.

Once I am locked in, Eugen hoists me up in the air by pulling the loose end of the rope. It launches me into the air by the hanger of the harness and I can't help but let out a little "Eep!"

"You ready yet?" Eugen asks me after he already launched me. His grasp on English is clearly above par. Barely. He flips the lever to lock the pulley in place effectively keeping me suspended in the air.

"Yes," I say to keep from rolling my eyes. If I'm rude he will wallop me in the shins with a hockey stick. He's a pain in the backside, but he's also a phenomenal coach and a dear friend. Plus, you only take a beating with a hockey stick so many times before you finally learn to hold your tongue. I guess Stepmonster should have taken some lessons for Eugen.

"Is good," he says as he turns to face us after he moves out of the way. "But your hand to hand lasso is not good."

The hand to hand lasso is one of the most widely recognizable lifts even if spectators do not know what it's called. Luc will lift me overhead by pressing up on his upturned palms. He'll rotate me as he lifts me and eventually we will be facing in the same direction. It's singlehandedly the lift that separates ice dancing from pairs figure skating as rules forbid the man from lifting the lady overhead—minus the jumps but who's judging.

Also, Eugen is correct in that we suck at it. Unfortunately, I think I know why. It's uncomfrotable for me to have a man other than Kane between my legs, even if it's business only. It's also something I'm going to have to get over and fast.

"Sophia, spread your legs," Eugen demands in his harsh accent. I was hoping Kane did not hear our instructions because he is standing behind the glass wall with his legs spread and his muscular arms folded across his chest, looks as if he heard every incendiary word.

And unfortunately, my theory is proven correct when he speaks.

"Excuse fucking me!" Kane roars.

I let out a sigh. It looks like this is going to be a

long morning.

"Close your mouth!" Eugen, not one to permit outbursts, shouts himself. "This is important."

"Yeah, Green," Luc taunts as he skates over to right underneath me and takes my hands in his and holds them right by my crotch. "This is important."

"Don't you freaking dare, Froglegs," Kane practically growls. Actually, scratch that. There is no practically about it. He. Is. Growling. Like an angry lion.

"It is not my fault that you do not know what you are doing between a woman's legs," Luc says as he presses his arms upward, lifting me above his head. Eugen pulls the ropes to lock me in place so that we can work on our form.

"Luc—" I try to warn him. This probably isn't the road we need to be going down right now. I need Luc and I to get through the Games before we can tackle any more life hurdles.

"Watch your mouth, Frenchman," Kane warns.

I'm trying to keep up with the escalation of conflict but between Eugen's rough Russian accent and Luc's subtle French one and I am at a complete loss.

"It is not really your fault," Luc says as if he's consoling a friend, but I know that he's doing anything but taunting Kane. "You Americans are so silly cutting the tips off of your penises. You simply can't be as good a lover as the French."

"Dude, you're Canadian." Kane rolls his eyes at Luc.

"I am French Canadian," Luc grumbles.

"Big difference, buddy," Kane bites out. "And a teeny tiny—and I do mean tiny—bit of foreskin on an eensy weensy dick doesn't make a damn bit of difference, Froglegs."

"You take that back!" Luc demands as he lets go of me and takes a menacing step towards Kane. I drop down a few inches before the harness catches me.

"Make me," Kane challenges. I can see the wheels turning in Luc's head and I know that whatever he says next is going to go over like a ton of bricks. And let me tell you, he does not disappoint.

"Maybe I'll just make the delectable Sophie come instead," he says with a wicked gleam in his eye and I gasp at his audacity.

In the time it takes me to blink Kane leaps over the lower glass partition and tackles Luc to the ice. The two of them roll and grapple as they each try to get the upper hand in the skirmish.

There is absolutely nothing I can do from up here but hangout—literally—and watch as Eugen tries to break up the fight. I am all but forgotten as I hang in the lift harness like a baby in one of those doorway jumpers.

They look like two cats wrestling.

Maybe I should get a cat. No, not until after this Olympic Cycle, of course, but a cat might be fun. Shelby and Trent seem to really love their cat, Missy. You know what's not fun? Hanging in this harness like a ragdoll.

"Guys?" I call out, but they completely ignore me. "Hey guys? I'm still up here."

Still nothing.

"Luc? Kane?" I shout but it's like I'm not even here. Maybe I should just take a nap until someone lets me down. They are so stupid. Well there's nothing I can do about it from up here. Where is Eugen anyways? He seems to have dissappeared somewhere.

Oh well, I give up.

"Good talk, guys."

FOUR

The Dog and Pony Show

"I trust you to do what needs to be done," my dad says as he shoots me with his glacial stare.

I let out a sigh. I know that I've developed a little bit of a reputation as a choke artist but still, coming from my dad it stings. And more than just a little.

My dad is supposed to be the one that always believes in me, the one who tells me that I can do anything that I set my mind to. He is supposed to tell me that there is nothing in this world that I cannot accomplish if I just want it bad enough to work hard enough for it.

But he's not.

That was my mom, and she's been gone for a long time.

My mom was the one who enrolled me in my first ice skating lesson at that very same rink in Del Mar when I was five. She told me that she just knew that I would look like a fairy princess on the ice. Before that, when I was two years old she signed me up for my first ballet class. She loved the diaper tutu combo and showed her polaroid pictures to anyone who wanted to see them.

Mom sat bundled up in her winter coat through every lesson whether after school or before dawn on a Saturday not like it was a duty, but like it was her profound honor to be there by my side. She videotaped performance run throughs so we could watch them and figure out what I was doing wrong. With every win she cheered the loudest, and every loss she cried the hardest.

I remember once, in seventh grade, after struggling all year with undiagnosed dyslexia, my mom and I sat in a parent teacher conference where my teacher, Mrs. Severs, told my mom that her faith in me while sweet was misguided. She told my mom that I was slow, and that I would never amount to anything in life. She had said that I would never go to college let alone graduate high school so my mom should stop wasting everyone's time demanding that they help me.

All while I silently listened to every damaging word that she spoke.

But my mom never believed her. In fact, she told her where she would go and that if she did not continue to work with me that we were going to the school board. My mom got me the help that I needed privately, and began succeeding in school with the right tools at my disposal.

She was so very proud of me.

And long after she passed away, I graduated high school and went on to finish college in three years, not four. I like to believe that my mom was watching over me every step of the way.

This year, I learned that my late step-mom, who was a Russian sleeper agent, had orchestrated the death of my mother so that she could take her place at my father's side while he climbed the political ladder all the way to the top. Oh, and to use me as whatever pawn she felt like in the moment while she was making my life a living hell.

Even after her death, my dad and I are still struggling to bridge the gap between us. I can only hope that one day he might come around. That he might find some value in me as a human being or a person he might want to know, and not as just a pawn to be used for his political gain. But even a Magic 8 Ball someone bought in the toy aisle at Target knows that outlook isn't so good.

Live and learn, right?

I hope.

About ten minutes after Luc and Kane decided to battle royale on the ice while I was left hanging there in a jump and lift harness my phone rang and thank Brian Boitano's one armed axel and all that's holy because it broke up the fight.

Both Kane and Luc freeze in their positions in the middle of their mid-ice grapple and turn their heads towards my phone ringing on the wall. They look a little like a couple caught in a backseat clinch by the cops on some Lover's Lane or Lookout Point makeout hotspot and the thought makes me giggle.

My first skating partner was a boy who got caught doing the naked foxtrot in the backseat of his boyfriend's car at a lookout point by his policeman older brother and his partner. Needless to say, his brother was pissed, and the partner handcuffed both my friend and his boyfriend naked while they stood there silently until his brother calmed down. His brother wasn't made that he was caught with a boy, he was mad that he felt someone was taking adantage of his baby brother. He had said he would be pised if it was a boy or girl but that no one got to mistreat his brother and get away with it. They are still close to this day and the two got married years ago. I heard they even adopted a baby this year. But needless to say, I can only assume that their faces at the time mirrored the guilty expressions of these two morons.

Kane immediately swings his head to stare at me.

"Is there something that you find funny, Tink?" he says, his voice rumbles low and ominous.

"No," I snicker. He narrows his eyes at me.

"Are you going to answer your phone?" Kane asks me.

"I would love to," I respond to his obviously stupid question while wondering if the old adage about stupid questions and stupid people is true. "But I'm a little tied up at the moment.

"I think I kind of like you all tied up," he purrs as he pushes up from the ice and jogs over to me to release the lever that is currently holding me in the air. Kane could let gravity take over and drop me down to the ice—goodness knows that that's probably what I would have done to him—but instead he lowers me gently, finally letting go of the rope when my blades touch the ice.

"Fantastic." I can't help but roll my eyes. "But now is not the time."

"If you two are done eye fucking each other," Luc snarks as I skate over to the wall and pick up my phone. I bite down on the fingers of my glove and pull my hand out so I can slide a fingertip across the screen to unlock it. "Can we get back to practice now?"

"Fuck you, Frenchie," Kane bites out.

"Sorry, but you're not my type," Luc snarks before turning to me. "Well? Practice, Sophie?"

I let out a sigh. "Actually, I can't. We've been summoned . . . well I have at any rate."

"What's going on?" Kane asks his body tensing as he goes instantly on alert.

"Oh, nothing much," I respond with another heavy

sigh. "I've been called to the carpet of the Senator's office so to speak."

"Yikes," Luc says while Kane eyes me with an intense scrutiny. "I don't envy you there."

"You don't have to come if you don't want to," I whisper feeling suddenly insecure. Gosh, I hate that feeling.

"Oh," he says, his voice rumbling with anger. "I'm going." And then he stalks off the ice.

"Well, alright then," I mumble mostly to myself before following after Kane.

"Hey," Luc says as he puts a hand to my elbow to stop me. "Are you going to be okay?"

I look him over to see if he's serious or just trying to make trouble for Kane and when I see the real concern on his face, I answer honestly. "Of course. It's Kane."

"Okay." He nods once before letting me go.

I stop in the team box and unlace my skates before wiping the blades down and covering them. I stow them in my skate bag and slide my feet into my sneakers. I zip my skate bag closed before standing from the bench. I reach for the handles of my bag and Kane swats them away with a gruff grunt before hauling it up to toss over his shoulder.

Kane takes my hand with his free one, and together we walk out of the rink. I have to blink a few times to clear the bright Southern California sunshine from my eyes. Kane beeps the locks on his truck with the key fob and pulls the passenger door open for me. He moves around the hood of the truck before pulling open the rear door and throwing my bag onto the back seat. Then slams the door closed before pulling open the driver's door and climbing in. He wears a scowl on his face as he cranks the engine over before turning to me to ask me the most ridiculous question.

"Is there something going on between you and Saucier that I should know about?"

"What?" I ask a little flabbergasted.

"Are you with Saucier?" he rephrases the question. "I have a right to know."

"No." I feel my face pull into a frown at the ridiculousness of his question. Whatever could he be on about now?

"No? No, I don't have a right to know?" he asks clearly getting upset and I jump to correct his wrong assumption.

"No! No, there's nothing going on," I say quick to clarify his jump to all the wrong conclusions.

"Why didn't you say so?" he asks softly.

"You just surprised me, that's all."

"Okay," he says to me before pulling out of the parking lot and head towards my dad's palatial home on La Jolla Scenic Drive.

"I mean it, Sophia," he warns.

"I know, Daddy." There is something about my dad and the way that he speaks to me that makes me feel so small and so young. And sadly, usually dumb and insignificant as well. After I almost died at the hands of my step-mom, his former wife, last year, I decided to prioritize my life. In doing so it led me to feel like this is no longer something I will accept—from my dad or anyone.

The minute we walked in the front door, I knew that there would be trouble.

"The Senator is in fine form tonight, Miss Sophie," Simmons had said to me as he pulled open the massive wooden doors for Kane and I to enter. "Good to see you again, Detective."

"Simmons." Kane smiled warmly to the butler that kept my insane upbringing as normal as possible.

"How bad are we talking here, Simmons?" I asked in hushed tones.

"Pretty bad, Miss." He nods solemnly. "They're talking campaign strategy."

"Oh, dear," I whisper conspiratorially.

"Agreed. Should I announce you?"

"No," I answered. "We'll see our way in."

"Very well then."

I laced my fingers through Kane's, closed my eyes, and took in a deep breath. I have to shore up my courage. If I have been summoned from practice for a political planning session, I am going to be three kinds of Tonya Harding mad.

"It'll be okay," Kane whispered into my ear to give me courage.

"Sure," I said after giving his hand a gentle squeeze.

I lead Kane through the house to the parlor where hushed voices could be heard but not loud enough that I could hear them from the other side of the door. I softly rapped my knuckles on the door before poking my head inside the room.

It's time to walk into the Lion's Den and here we are now . . .

"Hey, Daddy," I say as I walk fully into the room. "You wanted to see me?"

"Sophia, yes, I did. Come on in," he says to me by way of a greeting. Kane follows me into the room and I can tell that my dad's mood immediately sours. "Oh, hello, Detective. I wasn't expecting you."

"What can I say?" Kane says on a winning smile. "Where Sophia goes, I go."

"Well, isn't that just . . ." my dad trails off.

"Marvelous," I supply as an answer.

"Umm . . . yes," my dad says not wanting to look outwardly rude when he hasn't decided if he can use someone to his advantage or not yet.

"So, what was it you needed?" I ask. "It sounded important."

"Yes, it is," he tells me as he gestures towards the sofa. "Please, have a seat."

Together, Kane and I sit down on the sofa. He keeps my hand tucked neatly in his much larger one. This is a detail that doesn't escape my dad's notice by the way his eyes narrow ever so slightly where our hands rest on Kane's muscled thigh.

"Well, I'll just get right down to it," my dad starts without preamble. "I have decided to run for President of the United States."

Well, you could knock me over with a feather now.

Sweet Salchow, I did not see that one coming.

"But I thought you had decided against it after everything that happened . . ." I trail off. That everything encompasses the reign of terror that my father's second wife went on, one that almost led to my death.

"We've been going over the latest polls," my dad says gesturing between himself and his Majordomo of a campaign manager. "People find me relatable and highly likeable."

Well, I'm not sure how that happened. I mean he is just like everyone else, living in his gated mansion with his butler and his maid. I want to roll my eyes and somehow will myself not to.

The wonders never cease.

"Of course, you are," I hedge.

"Good," he says clapping his hands once as if everything has been decided. The hair on the back of my neck stands on end and I know, without a doubt, that I will absolutely hate whatever he says next. And he does not disappoint. "Now that you're onboard we need to go over your game plan."

"My game plan?" I repeat.

"Don't be obtuse, Sophia, it doesn't become you," he chastises me and Majordomo smirks at me behind his back.

"I'm not," I say softly and when he looks back at the papers in his hand, I take the break in his attention and flip her off. That feels better than anything I've done in a long time. She narrows her eyes at me and I smile even brighter. Kane chuckles softly over my shoulder.

"Oh yes," he says looking up. "Here we are." Then hands me a copy of the paper that he's looking at and I'm surprised—even shocked, maybe—although at this point in my life, I shouldn't be.

"Really, Dad?" I ask. "Marching orders?"

"Yes," he says to me firmly. "Everything for this campaign needs to be spelled out to the letter. You need to win the Olympics, Sophia."

"Well, I'm going to do my best," I tell him honestly.

"I mean it, Sophia," he warns.

"I know, Daddy."

"Don't let me down," he says with the weight of the world he is placing on my shoulders. "Don't let your country down."

"I'll do my best," I repeat my earlier statement. And it's true. I haven't been busting my tail only to land in Korea and get the pants beat off of me.

"Do better than your best," he orders and thank heaven that Kane is out of his line of sight because he definitely rolls his eyes at my dad.

"Okay." I can't help but feel a little beaten down right now. My dad steam rolls me at every opportunity and somehow, I just let him, *every time*. I'm hoping my dad will move on before he itemizes the rest of his demands on this list because those I will absolutely not agree to.

"When you get home," dad says, and I know that my terrible luck is still holding strong. "We'll talk about suitable political matches for you." I can feel Kane's frame stiffen next to me and the room goes wired but Dad doesn't seem to notice. Majordomo smiles openly now.

"Absolutely not," I say without even thinking to soften my response.

"Excuse me?" he roars softly.

"I said 'no'," I tell him. "You do not get to dictate my personal life."

"If it affects my campaign I do," he says sternly.

"No." I sigh before pressing on and feeling that gap between Dad and I widen even further. "The last time you tried to make a political match for me I almost died, and my career ended. You no longer have any say in my personal relationships."

"But we have it all planned out," he says unwilling to let go of his political machinations.

"I'm with Kane, Dad."

"You're going to marry a nice congressman like we had originally planned before Anderson and Annabelle screwed the pooch," Majordomo says before smiling like the cat that got the cream. "And I'm going to marry your father."

She wraps her arms around my Dad's waist and I have to fight back the urge to vomit or laugh at how absurd the entire thing really is. Laughter wins out. It starts as a snicker, maybe a giggle and bursts into huge belly laughs that have tears rolling down my cheeks.

"Really, Sophia?" she says snidely.

"Really," I choke out while trying to get a handle on my outburst. "And by really, I mean no. No, and hell no. None of those things are happening."

"You can't stop us," she challenges me.

"Dad, you can't love her," I say to him softly. "She's a total bitch."

"That's unkind, Sophia," Dad admonishes me, but he also doesn't disagree with the statement.

"It was." I smile at him. "But it was still true. Now, I'll address that ridiculousness item by item. First, I'm with Kane. I really care for him and he for me. That's not changing anytime soon. I am not marrying anyone to help your career. Not now, not ever. And second, if you marry her I will publicly support your opposing candidate."

"You wouldn't," she snarls.

"Try me."

"Sophia?" Dad asks.

"Really, she might be a good campaign manager, but she's awful. If you marry her, I'm out. She will be your new family and I will be with Kane."

"You can't mean that," he whispers.

"I do. It's time I started being more than an afterthought here," I tell him.

"But you already are," he whispers more.

"Then show me."

"But—" he starts.

"I'm with Kane, daddy."

He lets out a weary sigh. "Okay, but I still expect you to be on your best behavior when you're overseas."

"Of course." I smile at my dad.

"You can't let her get away with this!" Majordomo demands.

"I just did," my dad says firmly.

"Now, if you'll excuse us, I have to pack."

And with that I led Kane out of the parlor.

Something tells me that this won't be the last we hear of here, but it's like Rhett Butler once famously said, "Frankly, I don't give a damn."

FIVE

"Leaving' on a jet plane" and other semi-unfortunate surprises

"**W**h-what are you doing?" I ask as Kane whistles his way up the aisle of the Team USA plane.

"Like the song says," he answers me on a smirk while everyone around us looks on with obvious interest. "I'm 'leavin' on a jet plane.'"

"What?" I ask again.

"Surprise!"

Surprise is right, what the heck just happened here?

I came awake slowly.

The early morning gray of the California marine layer muted the sunlight that shone in the bedroom window. I could feel the hard heat of Kane curled in behind me. His face was buried in the crook of my neck and his lips were moving gently over my shoulder while the calloused pads of his fingers played between my legs.

"Kane," I gasped as I arched into his hand. I could feel myself already wet for him and already so close to that knife's edge of passion and bliss.

"That's it, Tink," his morning voice rumbled in my ear as he slid one finger deep inside me while his thumb swirled lazily around my clit.

"Kane, honey," I panted as he slowly pumped his finger in and out of me.

"That's my girl," he said as he added a second finger and I tipped my head back against his shoulder and moaned.

"Kane, I need you," I begged him.

"You've got me." His hand never letting up on its slow, sweet torture.

"Please."

"Please what, baby?" I could feel his mouth smile against my shoulder and I knew that he knew exactly what I needed but also that he wanted to hear me beg for him.

"Please. I need you inside me."

"I am inside you," he had said, and he emphasized that point by thrusting his fingers a little harder and a little faster inside me.

I also knew that I was going to have to say it out loud to get what I wanted but also that I was too far gone in my passion for him to care.

"I need your cock, baby," I had rasped. "I need it now, honey."

Just like that Kane slid his fingers from me and rolled me to my back in his bed. He straddled my closed legs and I reached for his hard length as it jutted out over my belly and wrapped my hand around it. I stroked him slowly as the sounds of crinkling foil filled the room before he gently brushed my hand away so that he could roll the latex ring down. I like to watch him do it, just as I always do. There's something about watching his fist slide down his shaft that I know without a doubt is hard for me. It gets me every time.

"I need you, baby," I whispered as his eyes locked with mine and he slid deep inside me.

"You have me, baby," Kane whispered to me in the quiet of the bedroom. "You always will."

He leaned down and touched his mouth to mine while never letting his eyes leave mine. Kane rocked his hips slowly against mine, slowly sliding his cock in and out of me.

"Fuck, you feel so good," Kane groaned against my mouth.

"Yes," I panted as he lit me up from the inside out.

"Love this pussy." He nipped at my ear before trailing his lips down the side of my neck. "Never had a pussy this sweet before."

I groaned and clenched around him at his dirty talk. It single handedly makes me blush and lights me on fire. I arch my back to rock into him as he slid his hands up my arms to lace his fingers with mine and hold them on either side of my head. With my legs and arms pinned by him I could do nothing but take whatever he was willing to give me, and it was so good while being so very bad.

He leaned forward a bit and took my nipple into his mouth and bit down while he pumped in and out of my body and I gasped.

"Kane," I had called out.

"That's it, baby," he said as he kissed his way back up my chest and neck until his mouth was on mine again, but this time is was different. There were no light touches and teasing. This time his tongue slid into my mouth like his cock slid into my pussy and overwhelmed my senses.

I squeezed his hands tighter in mine as he rocked his hips faster and faster. This time, Kane was going to give us what we both needed as he thrust harder and deeper, so deep he hit that spot that always made my toes curl.

"Oh God," I cried out as my nails bit into the tops of his hands.

"That's it," he said as he pumped his hips again and again. "Fuck, you're so tight the way you squeeze my cock when you come."

"Yes," I cry out. I'm so close that it almost hurts.

"I need you to let it go," he said on a strangled voice and I did just that. Kane tipped his head back on his shoulders and called out my name as he followed me over the edge.

He collapsed on top of me and we both laid there for who knows how long, our breaths sawing in and out of us, before either of us had moved or spoken. Kane finally broke the silence.

"Tink, you might just be the death of me."

"You woke me up," I reminded him.

"Yeah," Kane said, and I could hear the smile in his voice. "And then you fucked me within an inch of my life."

"Kane!" I shouted as my face heated to a bright red.

"That's cute," he whispered softly to me.

"What's cute?"

"It's cute when my good girl fucks me dirty and then gets embarrassed about it," he explained. I had covered my face with my hands before he spoke to me, which was ironic since his cock was still deep inside me. He gently pulled my hands away from my face. "Don't hide from me. I like everything about you."

"Some parts more than others," I said under my breath but by the flex of his hips he heard me.

"Yeah, those are some great parts," he chuckled.

"Kane!"

"Besides," he interrupted my yelling at him. "I'm surprised that you'd let me fuck you before you left. Most athletes say it's bad luck."

"What?!" I shouted. I had no idea what he was talking about. Bad luck?

"Yeah," he looked at me cautiously as if he was surprised that I didn't know. "It's bad luck to fuck before your event. Didn't you know?"

"No!" I shouted. "I was a virgin when you found me."

"Yeah," Kane agreed on a lazy smile.

"So how would I know that it was bad luck? Are you trying to get me to fail again?" I had begun to freak out.

"No, I was trying to get you to relax so that you don't lose it before you ever get to Korea," Kane explained and to be honest, it made a certain amount of sense. I was prone to freak out and then choke at the Games. "Plus, that's mostly for guys. We can't lose all of our testosterone before we go into battle."

"You know that sounds utterly ridiculous, right?"

"Kind of, but it worked," he said. "How's it working for you? Are you relaxed?"

I thought about it. "Umm . . . kind of."

"Kind of?" he asked me. "Well, then I guess we better get you into the shower, so I can make you more relaxed before you have to leave to catch your flight."

"Okay," I said because I liked the sound of Kane making me even more relaxed before I left for the airport.

So, I had let Kane lead me into the shower and do just that. By the time I was dressed in dark wash designer skinny jeans, my Team USA half zip pullover with my brand-new sneakers, my hair pulled into an artful ponytail and my makeup soft and sweet— I was totally relaxed with a lazy smile on my face and a natural blush on my cheeks.

"There's my gorgeous girl," Kane had said as he grabbed my bags and loaded them and me into his truck.

Kane drove me down to the airport where all of the Team USA athletes were given a private spot to say goodbye to their loved ones without the prying eyes of the media. After my bags were loaded on the plane, Kane wrapped me up in his arms and kissed me soundly.

"I'm going to miss you," I told him breathlessly.

There was a twinkle in his eye that I didn't quite trust.

"Nah, you'll be too busy to miss me," he responded.

"I'll never be too busy for you, Kane," I whispered, and his ice blue eyes turned to fire.

"You better get moving before you miss your plane," he said softly.

"I doubt they'll leave without us."

"Everyone else is boarding," he said and when I turned around, sure enough, everyone was filing onto the plane from the metal stairway on the side.

"I guess you're right," I said sadly.

"Don't worry, Tink. You'll be seeing me sooner than you think," he said.

"Okay."

And with one last kiss I turned and walked away. I walked up the metal staircase and to the seat on my ticket—which was not next to Luc or anyone else. How weird. I buckled my seatbelt and leaned my head back and shut my eyes. Maybe I'd sleep most of this flight. We had plenty of hours in the air ahead of us.

I have no idea how long I sat there waiting for the plane to take off when I realized that all conversations around me had stopped.

Then I heard a familiar voice singing an old John Denver tune and I knew that I had been had.

"Wh-what are you doing?" I ask as Kane whistles his way up the aisle of the Team USA plane.

"Like the song says," he answers me on a smirk while everyone around us looks on with obvious interest. "I'm 'leaving' on a jet plane.'"

"What?" I ask again.

"Surprise!"

"You're on this flight?" I ask as he settles into the seat next to mine.

"Yep." Kane smiles brightly. "I pulled some strings and took some time off of work. After that case with the missing hookers that Shelby and Daisy stumbled upon they were happy to give me some vacation time to cheer on my girl."

"That's great," I said, and I meant it.

I relaxed into my seat and settled in for the long flight. I suddenly wasn't nervous at all because I knew that I had Kane's strength to see me through. Everything was going to be just fine.

Too bad everything would go to crap in just a few days, but how was I to know?

SIX

Adultery and the Olympic Flame

The Parade of Nations and the Opening Ceremony are some of my favorite parts of the Games. The emotions and the expectations are so palpable and hope and national pride flow through everyone. The air is literally shimmering with excitement and you can feel it all around you.

After several layovers, our plane finally landed in South Korea. Unfortunately, that meant we—the Team USA athletes and myself—only had a short amount of time to check into the Olympic Village and prepare for the Opening Ceremonies.

I'm rooming with some girl from the ladies hockey team. She keeps asking me about my relationship with Kane and I'm not sure if it's because she's interested in me or him and wants to feel out how serious it is between us. She's bubbling over with mid-western naivete and charm. So much so that it makes me feel bad for trying to brush her off. I'm not here to make friends, I am here to win a title and if she was serious about her hockey career, she would be too.

I politely declined to answer her questions and changed into my Opening Ceremony uniform that we all have. I brush and curl my hair and do my makeup darker than normal but still in sweet colors. I wrap my scarf around my neck and pull a knit cap down over my blonde curls and head for the door.

Luc is waiting for me at the door with his hand poised to knock when I swing it open.

"Ready to go?" he asks me without missing a beat.

"Of course!" I tell him before looking back to my roommate before bolting out of the room. "See you there!"

Luc and I walk through the village to the staging area for the Parade of Nations. What we did not do is invite my roomie to join us. I feel guilty about excluding her from our fun but, like I said, I'm not here to make friends. If I can't focus now, I won't be able to later and that is when it really counts. I need to keep my head in the game. This is my last chance.

We join the rest of Team USA as each country takes their places in the lineup. Team USA is behind France and in front of Germany as we begin our walk through the village and into the stadium. People stop when they see us to take pictures or shout for their nation. It's an amazing experience.

I whip my cellphone out of my pocket and start

taking pictures and videos too. Luc reaches over and hits the button to flip the camera around so we can snap a couple of selfies while we walk in the parade and the whole thing makes me laugh at the ridiculousness of it. But at the same time, I needed it. I have put so much pressure on myself to be the best that I can and if I don't have a little fun and let off some steam I might crack. Luc seems to understand that about me and I will forever be grateful.

Luc looks over his shoulder and smirks. I roll my eyes at his saucy stare and look over to see what or who he might be watching. He is such a playboy. Luc's single man antics are ridiculous. And as it turns out he's watching one of our competitors, Layla Wagner, of Germany—our very *married* competitor.

He slows us down letting other members of Team USA pass us in the lineup so that we end up at the back near Team Germany. Layla weaves her way up to the front of her pack as well. A burning pit opens up in my stomach. I always knew that Luc was a wild card, but Oksana Baiul on a balance beam, I was hoping to get through this competition before he made trouble for himself—*and me.*

"Hello there, handsome," she purrs from behind us in her heavily accented voice. It's like a Merlena Dietrich kind of effect—a little sexy, a little authoritarian. Maybe that's just the German way. I don't really know.

"Hello, Layla. You're looking lovely as ever," Luc says as if they have known each other for year. And maybe they have. I don't really know Luc all that well. Maybe she knows him better. That thought turns my stomach sour with anxiety.

"So are you," she coos in a voice full of sexual promise.

"Looks like we need to get moving," I say hoping to distract them but like everything else in my life, my efforts fall flat.

"I'd love to see if the rumors are true," she says to Luc. "That is if you can shake Miss Do-Good."

"Hey," I say and Luc laughs. I'm not going to lie, it stings a little that my own partner does not jump to my defense but instead jokes at my defense with his potential paramour. My gut reaction is to walk away, but the last thing I need to do with with world watching is to cause a scene.

"I'm in room 430 of the village. Johan won't be there tonight," she whispers conspiratorially.

"What about your husband, Johan?" I ask her wanting to drive the conversation to highlight her marital status.

Layla lets out a husky laugh. "Johan will find other pursuits to keep him busy and even if he doesn't," she adds with a wink. "He takes a double dose of Ambien every night. He can't sleep without it but he's dead to the world once it hits him. So . . . while he sleeps in the bed, Luc and I can find another . . . surface . . . to occupy for a little while."

"I have seen my fair share of coat closets," Luc

comments on a laugh and Layla joins him as if he is the most entertaining man in the world.

"Oh gross," I say under my breath. I can't believe they would be so bold as to have relations in the same room as her sleeping husband.

Poor Johan.

I would hate to be saddled with someone as selfish and manipulative as Layla. The thought reminds me to reinforce my emotional shields and not let my dad and his Majordomo con me into making a political match and marrying someone I do not love for the sake of his political career. As great as I think my dad would be for our country if he held the highest office, I will not be the one to make the sacrifices it takes to put him in the Oval Office. I was serious when I told them that I am with Kane and I plan to stay that way for a good long while. And lately, I hope that maybe, just maybe, we might be together for the rest of our lives.

"I'll see if I can make it." Luc winks at her obviously unwilling to be derailed by logic or even a moral compass.

"See that you do," she says, trailing her dragon talon of a fingernail down his chest before popping it back up to tap the tip of Luc's nose before making her way back into the Team Germany crowd.

"Luc!" I admonish him quietly. "I can't believe you!"

"What?" he laughs.

"What do you mean 'what'?" I whisper shout at

him. "You know 'what' and you know that she is our competitor. *Her and her husband.*"

"So what?" he shrugs his shoulder at me.

"So, you shouldn't be messing around with her!" I can't believe this. Luc is not taking this nearly serious enough.

"Calm down," he says on a laugh.

"Calm down, calm down!" I can hear myself freaking out and yet I am so far gone down the panic rabbit hole that there is no way to pull myself out of it. "This is serious!"

"They give out all those condoms for a reason, pet," Luc says softly as if that is all that he needs for permission to be a complete cad.

"Kane said it's bad luck to have sex before you compete," I try to convince him otherwise.

"So, you didn't let him touch you this morning?" he asks me with a knowing look in his eyes.

"That's different."

Luc smirks. "How so?"

"He said it's bad luck for men," I explain. "And he's not our competitor."

"Are you sure that's true?" He asks me.

"Yes. Kane's career on the ice is over."

"That's not what I asked you," Luc says softly.

"She's married." I try again.

"So what? Marriage is just a piece of paper," he tries to explain his reasoning and I can't help but wonder what happened to him that made him have no re-

spect for marriage, or any marriage at that.

"You really instill confidence in the institution," I say rolling my eyes.

"So then don't get married." He shrugs his shoulders as if it's no skin off his nose whether I get married or not.

"I'm not," I inform him haughtily.

"Tell that to Mr. You-Banged-My-Bitch-of-a-Wife," Luc says as he nods his head toward the family seats in the front row of the arena. I spot Kane watching, more importantly, he's watching me, not the Parade of Nations. His eyes are only for me in a way that sends sparks down my spine and heat in uncomfortable places seeing as we're in front of forty thousand people.

"Kane doesn't want to get married," I say turning back to Luc but suddenly I'm not so sure.

"I'm not so sure about that," Luc responds, echoing my very same thoughts and even I have to admit that the way that Kane looks at me is like I am everything he needs to survive, like I hung the moon and the stars in the sky just for him. And maybe if I could, for him, I would.

"Are you really going to hook up with Layla?" I ask breaking the silence between us as I turn back to look at Luc.

Johan makes his way over to us and for a minute I brace thinking that there is going to be a fight between Luc and Johan. I wonder if he's the kind of man to defend his wife's honor and their marriage even though she clearly doesn't deserve it. I know without a doubt that Kane would fight anyone that he had to, including me, to protect our relationship from outside forces and we're not even married. Johan and Layla have been married for thirteen years.

I shouldn't have worried so much because it appears that Johan could care less about Luc and whatever it is he plans to do with Johan's wife. It would also seem that our German competitor has his sights set on me. *Oh, dear*. I should have been paying more attention.

"Hello, darling," he purrs into my ear as he places his body uncomfortably close to mine. "It's so nice to see some fresh meat here."

I don't remind him that this is my third time at the Games and only my first—and probably last—in pairs skating. When I don't respond to him, but only try to move away from him he grabs me and pulls me tightly to him.

"Now, don't be rude, *Kleine Mous*," he says. I know just enough German to know that he has called me Little Mouse, a pet name after being in my presence for approximately two seconds. I don't like it one bit. "We should get together tonight."

"No, thank you," I decline. "I'm involved with someone."

"He doesn't have to know," Johan says on a laugh. "After all, I'm not planning on telling my wife. Not

that she'd care anway. She has plans to fuck your partner."

I hate his use of crude language in front of me. I'm
almost always uncomfortable with curse words, except
when Kane uses them in the good ways, but otherwise
I don't like it at all. I try to pull away from him again
but he still won't let me go. There is just something
about this man that sets my teeth on edge.

"I said 'no, thank you' and I meant it," I say in low
tones, not wanting to draw any undue attention to us.
You never know who may be watching you at these
events and it is always wise to put your best foot forward. Clearly, Johan sis not get the memo.

"Stupid move, *Kleine Mous*, I am not a man that
you want to disappoint," he warns in angry tones. "I
am going to be the next Olympic Champion."

"We'll just see about that," I say on a false smile.
It feels to bright and too false on my face. "I am afraid
that I'm going to have to take that risk, I am very much
attached to my boyfriend and I don't waste my time
with men who could not possibly compare to him."

"You'll be sorry, bitch," he says with a parting shot
before flouncing back the way he came and I have to
say good riddance.

"Thanks for your help there," I say in a snide voice
that I instantly hate. "I really appreciated it."

"You didn't look like you needed me," He says.

"You're absolutely right," I say. "I didn't need you
when he held me against my will and I didn't need you

to defend me while he threatened me but then again why would you when you're too busy worrying about the logistics of your rendezvous with his tramp of a wife."

Luc looks away from me for a minute and I think that I know his answer. Luc is one of those guys that will hit you head on with the truth whether you want to know it or not. He's a lot like Kane in that way. So, if he is avoiding my eyes for any reason, he knows that I won't approve of what he wants to do. I can only surmise that means it's not a what but a who and that who is Layla Wagner.

"Word on the street is if they don't win here, it's over between them—on and off the ice," he says after a moment of thinking to himself.

"What?" I gasp. That can't possibly be true. Layla and Johan are the Torvill and Dean of our generation. They are the pride of Germany and everyone loves them because they so obviously love each other. Although, I guess that can't be true if she is setting up liaisons with other skaters all around the world.

"It's true." He sighs and runs a hand through his perfect hair. "She's done with him."

"Poor guy." I know what it's like to have others find you sorely lacking in one way or another. I guess I can relate to him after all even if he is a creep.

And it makes me like Layla even less than I did before.

"Yeah," Luc agrees with me and sort of diffusing

the situation between us.

I wish Luc wouldn't get involved with her. But I guess that's for him to decide and not me.

Maybe I should arrange a liaison for myself, Kane, and thirty-two condoms . . .

SEVEN

Moves in the field and Moves on my person

I don't know whether or not Luc went to Layla last night and I don't care. That is as long as he shows up to our practice on time. Aside from that, I think I have to let my feelings on the situation go. I wish he wouldn't entertain her, but at the same time, it's none of my business and he clearly does not care about my opinions and feelings on the matter either.

Basically, Luc will do Luc and I'll do me and I can only hope that he is as interested in pursing a Gold medal over Layla's person.

We only have so many official practices before we skate the short program portion of the competition. Freaking Sonja Henie's ice skates, I hope he shows up. I can't skate this practice alone. Well, I could but it would be super awkward. Then again, so am I so what else is new?

This practice is one that four teams will skate on

the ice at the same time. We have no music but we will have access to the rink to feel it out. The judges may also be present, you just don't know who they are. In fact, you never know who may be watching so it's all about smiles and false confidences.

Fake it until you make it and all that.

Spectators may also observe these practices even though they are less exciting and much less flashy than the actual competitions. I spy Kane is in the stands and seeing him eases a little of the tension in my body. Even if I didn't recognize him right away, I would know that he's here. There's an energy that connects Kane and I. I come to life when he's near. It's like I was living in a muted world and the minute he's near colors are brighter and music is sweeter.

He's wearing jeans and a heavy winter coat. Covering his sandy brown hair is a Team USA knit cap. But not the one from this year's line—it's the one from his year at the games and I absolutely love that. I love that he's held onto it for decades. I love that he brought it out to be here to support me. Sweet Salchow, I love Kane.

It's five o'clock in the morning here in Korea and I'm tired and grouchy. I got up this morning and dressed in a practice dress which is more than a basic dress with a little glitz and glamor but not as much as the dress I will wear for the actual competition, and also tights, and a sweater. I had breakfast of fruit, yogurt, and one cup of coffee in the dining hall at the

Olympic Village where Eugen looked very unhappy to not find Luc also ready to get in the van to head to the rink. I had just shrugged my shoulders when he looked at me with those knowing eyes and then we got in the van and headed to the rink designated for figure skating competitions.

My skates are laced up and I'm stretched out with my body warmed up. I have earbuds in and my phone playing an oldie but a goodie, *You Gotta Be* by Des'ree. I let the piano and her words flow over me as I shake out my arms and get ready to step on the ice. I remember my very first coach had me listen to this song to pump myself up and get out of my own head before my first solo competition. It has become a tradition ever since.

Besides, the last thing I want to hear is the other teams talking about my missing in action partner and trying to shake me up. Competitions at this level are half talent and hard work and half mental warfare. You have to stay strong and raise up those mental shields that could survive a nuclear blast in order to survive here.

This level of competitive skating is cut throat. Before we left the dressing room, I heard the French skater saying she couldn't find her skates. She had just left them in their bag to run to the restroom for a second and when she returned to her locker room, they were gone. And as awful as it sounds, I'm not even surprised. It's why I guard my skates and my dress like silver in Fort

Knox. I have seen girls place broken glass in someone else's skates or change the blades on the boot.

But what does catch my eye is the wicked gleam in Layla's eyes as the French skater cries and cries. This was her only official practice too and Layla effectively removed her from the game. Layla cuts her gaze to me and I lock eyes with her in an effort to show her that I see exactly who she is, and I am not impressed.

After that she disappeared, and I headed out to wait to enter the ice. I did not see Layla again, nor did my wayward partner show up. So, who knows what is actually going on here? It's any man's guess.

Eugen places a gentle but strong hand on my shoulder to let me know that the official from the International Olympic Committee or IOC has opened the gate and teams are taking the ice. I press pause on my music app and wrap my earbud cords around my phone and hand it to Eugen. He tucks it into his coat pocket as I unzip my Team USA sweater and hand it to him as well.

I look around, one of the French and one of the Russian teams are already on the ice showing off their moves. I feel the hair prickle on the back of my neck and look over my shoulder. Johan is standing off to the side with his arms folded over his chest. When his eyes meet mine, he steps forward to move towards me, and I panic.

I don't want to draw attention to the fact that my partner and his wife are probably burning up the sheets again and we stand here looking like complete fools. So, I throw my arms wide with a flourish and step onto the ice.

If Luc doesn't have the common decency to show up at our official practice, then I will do my best to show that I've got this. I run through some complicated elements, not necessarily the ones in our short program, I don't want to give away my hand until Luc and I kill it in the competition. That is if he even shows up for that one either.

And if he doesn't, I'll kill him. Slowly.

I look up into the stands and see Kane watching me intently. Smiling for all to see as he sits proud in the stands watching me. He looks up from signing someone's program and waves to me with the hand that's still holding one of those big, fat permanent markers that smell terrible. I wave back before changing direction.

I run through all of the complicated jumps and jump combos that I can. I land every single one of them and feel on top of the world. Even without my no-good lounge lizard of a partner here, I look good, making us look good and the other competitors see it. That's all that matters.

I feel strong arms wrap around me in a basic hold and I look up to see Luc looking very upset. He leads me through different sections of our routine and a couple of extras to keep the others guessing before he finally speaks to me.

"Don't be mad," he says, and it has the opposite of his desired effect on me. I am very angry with him, but I would never show it here. That I will save for behind closed doors.

"Don't make a scene," I respond in low tones. "Let's just get through this practice and we'll talk somewhere private later."

"I'm sorry," Luc says softly. And I want to believe him, but I just don't.

"Don't ruin my career," I whisper back.

"Okay," he says softly.

"Okay," I agree and I let it go—for now.

Luc took my hand and led me through one series of complicated elements after another. We worked hard and ran through everything over and over again. I was sweating when the buzzer sounded to tell us that our time was over, and we exited the ice.

What we didn't do was talk about what happened, a mistake I would regret in the coming days.

EIGHT

He wants your autograph and other life altering lies

"**H**earts all over the world are a twitter for the budding romance between former U. S. Hockey Olympic player Kane Green and the current US Pairs Figure skater Sophia Dubois. Green was seen observing yesterday's open pairs practice," *a male sports commentator says on the television.*

"Looks like tongues are wagging for you and Green," my roommate says and I can't help but wonder why she is so interested.

"It's not all that it's cracked up to be," I say quietly.

"That's right, Rick," *the female commentator to his left says.* "Witnesses say the former gold medalist only had eyes for America's Sweetheart leaving fans wondering if a post-Games proposal might be in the works."

"Dude," my roommate says, and I think not for the first time that I should really learn her name. "Are you guys getting married?"

"No," I scoff. "Of course not."

"Dubois was the front runner for the Ladies' Singles competition when an injury took her out of the running," *the man says.*

"That's right," *the woman agrees.* "She was viciously attacked by her fiancé and step mother."

"Talk about family problems!" the man laughs as if there is anything funny or charming about the story of how I almost died at the hands of the people that I trusted the most. *"Now here's the weather with Amy. Isn't she great everyone!"*

"Wow," my roommate says on a slow blink. Honestly, she looks a little stunned. "That seems . . . *rough.*"

"Yeah," I agree. "It really was."

We sit there are stare at the TV for I don't know how long until the ringing of my phone breaks me free from my thoughts. Without looking at the caller ID on my phone, I swipe my finger across the screen to unlock my phone.

"Hello?" I answer and as soon as the voice on the other end of the line responds, I immediately regret that I did.

"Sophia!" my dad screeches. "What the hell are you doing with that man?"

"Dad." I sigh. "I already told you that Kane and I are together. You know this."

"The news is saying that you are engaged," he barks into the phone. "Tell me that even you could not be that stupid." Wow, that didn't hurt at all. Here comes Sophie, choke artist ad all around screw up again. Huzzah!

"Well, the news is wrong," I tell him honestly. "I am not engaged—to Kane or to anyone else."

"Let's just keep it that way," he growls, and I can't help but roll my eyes. How they still think that they have any say in the rest of my life, I do not understand at all.

"Sure, Dad," I say trying to ease the tension. I mean really, I'm here to compete at the Olympics for Pete's sake, not to find a husband. I can't help but wonder how much trouble he thinks I can get into. Which when I stop and think about it really makes me mad because I have never done anything bad in my entire life. I have done nothing but try my best to be the perfect daughter and sadly, it was never enough for him.

Not that marrying Kane would be bad either. I have had a lot of time to think about what my life might be like when these Games are over. I am going to have the whole world ahead of me with open possibilities and the more that I think about it, the more that I want Kane there with me for the next adventure, whatever that might be.

"Stay out of trouble!" my dad clips out before he disconnects. I look at my phone and blink before hitting the lock button on the side.

"Everything okay?" my roommate asks.

"Yeah," I lie. "Just peachy."

"And I thought hockey was bloody," she mumbles more to herself than anyone else, but I hear her anyways and besides, she's not wrong.

I let out a sigh just as my phone rings again. This time I take a moment to look and see who it is and speak of the devil, it's Kane.

"Hey, handsome," I answer.

"Hey, Tink," he says, and I can hear the smile in his voice. "Do you have any free time today?"

"It just so happens that I do," I tell him and it's the absolute truth even if I want to run away from my life for a bit. Luc is off again with Layla. Even though I think that he's being a bonehead that doesn't mean that he's going to stop doing what he's doing. Either way, I need to get out of this room and out of my head and a little rendezvous with Kane is just the solution.

"Fantastic," he says. "I'll meet you at the bus stop in an hour."

"Sounds good. I'll see you then," I say before disconnecting.

I jump up in a flurry of activity. I grab clothes out of my suitcase and change into dark skinny jeans and a sweater with a deep cowl neck that is a shade somewhere between cream and off white. I wear a lace trimmed tank of the same color underneath. I wrap a wide brown leather belt around my hips and tuck my feet into tall leather riding boots that match.

I take up the bulk of my remaining time curling my hair so that it looks like I didn't do anything to it at all, but it's so thick and so long that it takes a long time to do. When I'm done I tap a little soft pink blush on my cheeks and do my eye makeup in soft, shimmery browns. I top it off with a touch of pink gloss on my lips which I tuck into my small, pink leather handbag. Lastly, I push my mom's diamond earrings through my ears and wrap her watch around my wrist.

"Wow," my roommate says. "I didn't know it was possible to girly girl that fast."

I can't help but let out a laugh. "Well, I've had years of practice. I'll show you later if you'd like."

"Yeah, I think I would," she says softly. "There's a guy on the men's team. He doesn't notice me."

"Then he's an idiot," I say softly. "But most men are."

"He plays pro," she says a little sadly. "He's got loads of puck bunnies back home."

"Now, I know he's an idiot," I tell her gently. "But I want to hear more about this guy when I get back tonight. Then we'll see if we can't puzzle it out while I teach you some basic makeup tricks."

"I'd like that."

"Me too."

And then I left to meet Kane at the bus stop, slipping my heavy winter coat on over my clothes as I walked out the door and tossing my small purse over my shoulder.

I wind my way through the Olympic Village before I end up at the bus stop. Kane is there, leaning casually against the street lamp. His smile brightens when he sees me.

"Ready to blow this popsicle stand?" he asks me as he offer me his arm.

"Definitely."

"Then let's go."

"Where, exactly, are we going?" I ask.

"That part is a surprise."

"Is it that penis park?" I ask, and Kane barks out a laugh.

"No." He smiles at me. "Why do you ask?"

"Because Verna and Marla would be so upset if we saw it without them," I explain.

"And you think your dad would mind if you were seen in a penis park?"

"Heavens no!" I laugh. "But at this point I just don't care. Now, I'm living my life before it passes me by."

"Can I be a part of this life living?" he asks and there's a weight to the question in his voice as if it holds more meaning than simple conversation.

"I wouldn't want anything more," I say softly.

"Good." Then he leans down and brushes his lips over mine.

A woman with a basket over her arm full of flowers for sale walks by and Kane stops her, conversing fluently with the woman. I'm impressed. He picks out a lovely bouquet about the size of a navel orange and pays for it with money he slips from his front pocket.

She smiles at him and hands Kane the flowers before moving on. Kane walks back over to me and presents the flowers to me on a bow. I can't help but smile at his playful behavior.

"Thank you," I say as I smell the sweet blossoms.

"Anything for my girl."

"I'm impressed," I admit to him. "I didn't know that you spoke Korean."

"Yeah," he laughs. "I forget about it and then it just pops out of my mouth like I never stopped."

"When did you learn? Or really where?" I ask as we keep walking through the park.

"I had a roommate when I was just starting out in the International League," Kane says. "He was a giant kid and spoke absolutely no English. As we became friends I taught him English and he taught me Korean. His mom still sends me treats on my birthday."

"That's sweet," I tell him.

"Hey look," he says pointing to a building of the beaten path. "It's a tea house."

"That sounds nice."

Kane leads me by the hand through the side alleyway. The sun is setting as he walks through the door of the small tea house. Another woman greets us as we walk in and leads us to a private room towards the back of the building. She talks openly with Kane and I get the feeling he told her that I don't understand what she's saying.

She smiles at me before saying something to Kane. He turns to me to translate. "She says you're very beautiful."

"Thank you."

The woman takes our coats from us and hangs them on hooks by the door before leaving. Kane walks over to me and hugs me. He's not a hugger, but this has been a special day. I'll take it.

A man about Kane's age walks in followed by the older woman who greeted us at the door. The man hugs Kane and slaps his back in that way that men do, and I find the whole things fascinating.

"Kane?" I ask softly.

"Sophie, these are friends," he tells me.

"Okay," I say for lack of a better response.

"This is Se Jun and his mother, Mi Na," Kane explains. "These are the friends I was telling you about."

He goes on to say something to them about me.

"I thought you said this was a tea house?"

"It is." He smiles that snake charmer smile at me and I can't help but think that Kane is up to something. I smile back to throw him off his game. Whatever he's up to, I'll find out soon enough. I was telling the truth when I said I'm living my life while I still can.

Se Jun and Kane speak openly and very friendly, I only wish that I could understand what they are saying as Mi Na pours tea from a beautiful china service.

"Se Jun is a huge fan," Kane says turning to me and it looks as if everyone is holding their breath. I wonder why. "He wants to know if you're going to win."

I smile brightly and hope that I'm telling the truth. "Yes."

Se Jun says something else to Kane and answers in what I can only assume is the positive of whatever he had asked him. Odd that Korean citizens are cheering for American athletes, but who am I to judge anyways? I need all the luck I can get—especially with my partner off who knows where doing who knows what with who knows whom.

Kane says something else to Se Jun and he flashes his eyes to me before responding to Kane. Kane looks over his shoulder to me before saying, "He'd really like an autograph, can you come sign this paper for my buddy, Se Jun?"

"Of course," I tell him. "Any friend of Kane's is a friend of mine."

Kane smiles broadly as I sign the paper but Se Jun is looking a little ill. He pulls at the collar of his shirt and his forehead is covered with sweat.

"I don't think Se Jun is doing so well, honey," I whisper to Kane.

"I think you're right," Kane agrees as he takes me into his arms and kisses me on the lips. Odd behavior for someone worried about his friend. "I'm sure he'll be alright after he gets some rest."

"Oh okay."

Kane ushers me over to a beautiful table and holds a seat out for me. Mi Na serves tea and delicious treats as we sit and visit with her for awhile. As it turns out, Se Jun is the youngest of her children and she has 7 grandchildren who all think Kane hung the moon.

We stayed for hours before walking out into the night only to find that the temperatures had dropped to below freezing and that it was sleeting. The streets were empty. Everyone must be hiding out for this winter storm that seems to have come from nowhere.

"We should find a place to wait out the storm," Kane says to me.

"Alright," I tell him as I place my hand in his. "Lead the way."

Kane magically finds a gorgeous boutique inn a block down from Mi Na's tea house. He checks us in to a small room with a tiny bed covered in pink silk sheets and a window that overlooks the park. By the time we get settled inside, I am absolutely freezing.

Kane slowly strips us of our wet clothes piece by piece. It's almost a slow seduction and not the fast rip and tug one would associate with shedding soaked clothes. Each new patch of skin revealed is more exciting than the next and I get a quick glimpse of his desire for me as it juts out from his body before Kane pulls back the covers on the bed and he gently lays me down in the middle before covering me with his own body and pulling the covers up over us.

He trails his hands all over my body infusing heat into me that I thought was gone for good with the onset of the winter winds and freezing rain. Sparks zing across my skin with each new touch and caress. After a moment I'm warm all over, especially when he touches his mouth to mine. When his tongue slips into my mouth, I'm burning up from the inside out.

I need Kane and I need him now.

He slowly parts my thighs and I'm eager to accommodate him as Kane reaches over to his jeans on the floor and pulls a condom from his pants pocket. He lets the material fall back to the lush carpet before tearing open the packet and rolling the latex down his hard length.

I wrap my arms around his shoulders when he settles his weight back over me and hold him tight when he covers me with his body again. When he slides deep inside I get lost in him and me and in this stolen moment that we have together.

Kane swallows my cries into his mouth with each press of his body into mine. The slow, gentle rock of his hips into mine drives me higher and higher. We don't talk, we only feel each other and this connection that we have as his body slides in and out of mine in a rhythm as old as time.

I cling to him for dear life as my climax washes over me and whisper his name, "Kane."

Kane thrusts inside me once . . . twice . . . three times more before groaning out his own climax as he follows me over the edge. He stays rooted inside me for as long as he can, our breaths mingling as we hold each other in the quiet room.

Kane alternates between holding me in his arms and making love to me twice more throughout the night as the snow falls outside the window and there is nowhere else that I would rather be.

Too bad that tomorrow, I would find out that sometime during the night, everything had changed . . .

NINE

Bonnie and Clyde

Two days later . . .

I lean against the vanity top in the bathroom back in the Olympic Village and dust a rosy blush on my cheeks.

Yesterday was a media nightmare. Luc and I had one press junket after another and each reporter asked an inappropriate question after another more inappropriate question. It was like they were trying to one up each other on who could ask the most outlandish things.

The cat was officially out of the bag on Luc and Layla and their illicit affair. That's up to him to deal with so I let him handle those questions, but when the topic turned to my dad and his career and the fact that Kane and I spent the previous night together, I was less than amused.

After our first round of interviews, Luc and I had

one last official practice before the short program skate, and we bombed like Tonya Harding. It was so bad. He dropped me three times and we couldn't get our timing down to save our lives.

As of last night, it looked like my awesomely horrific record of being an Olympic choke artist is holding out. Which was also the topic of conversation at our second press conference. Needless to say, I did not sleep well last night. At one point in time, I wished that I had one of Johan's Ambien pills even though that's not my style.

This morning, I received a text message from Kane telling me to "break a leg" and it was then that I knew that I was screwed. That's one of those things that figure skaters never say before a competition, so I know that my run of bad luck is holding strong. So, I resigned myself to do the best that I could. It's not over until the fat lady sings and all that jazz.

So, I dressed in sweats and had a healthy breakfast by myself. I curled my hair and styled it in a 1920's style with a beaded headband before starting my make-up. The stage makeup is the worst part of competitions. You basically slather it on with a trowel. I absolutely hate the look of it on my face, but it looks great on the ice. And the fact that my skin is green, and I could yak at any moment doesn't show. So, there is a silver lining somewhere. Yippee!

I strip out of my sweats—careful not to mess up my makeup or hair—and then roll my brand-new tights up my legs. I can't wear anything underneath or it will show. I put my blush pink 1920's style dress on. It has a vee cut in the front and back but is otherwise fairly modest. It has a soft flowy skirt that hits at my calves in the back and my knees in the front, but its deep slit lets the material float like wings while we skate. The bodice is covered in crystals and pearls. The whole thing is absolutely gorgeous and fits our Bonnie and Clyde theme.

I pull my Team USA warm up over my dress and slide my feet into my favorite chucks. I swipe one last swish of pink lipstick across my mouth before shoving the tube into my skate bag and sling it over my shoulder.

"Hey bitch," my roommate, Natalie, says when I reach for the door.

"Yeah?" I ask as I pause at the door.

"You got this," she says as she holds two thumbs up towards me as she smiles brightly.

"Thanks." I shoot her a smirk over my shoulder as I head out the door, because yeah, I do.

No one is going to make this happen but me and my French-Canadian man-ho of a partner. So, let's do this.

A golf cart and driver are waiting to take me to the rink. I hop on and take a deep breath. I take it all in. I don't want to miss a moment of this. This is my last Games, my last chance.

We pull up to the back entrance of the rink and I

climb down from the golf cart.

"Thank you," I tell the driver on a smile.

"Good luck," he says before driving off.

I walk through the back of the rink and tune out everyone else. It's weird to say because the backstage area is crawling with people, but I can't focus on any of them. This moment right here is just for me and my headspace as I move through the crowd.

Eugen and Luc find me. Eugen is in a gray suit with a white shirt and a black straight tie. He looks fantastic and not at all like the crazy Russian who hits my knees with a hockey stick when they aren't bent deep enough. The two sides of him make me laugh and through it all I know that he truly cares about me and my success.

Luc is wearing brown tweed slacks and a light pink shirt with a pink straight tie and brown suspenders. He tops it all off with a brown fedora style hat. He's rocking the Bonnie and Clyde era too and I think it came off really well.

Together, we head to our dressing area. I strip off my warm-ups while Luc stretches. I join him before we walk through our routine a few times in our stocking feet.

"You looks good," Eugen says. I'm a little shocked because he's never offered me any kind of compliment before. "Time to put skates on."

Luc and I sit side by side on a bench as we lace up our skates. Luc takes a deep breath and pushes up from the bench before offering me a hand.

"Let's go kick some ass, shall we?" he asks me as he holds out his hand for me to take.

"Yes, let's," I say on a smile as I place my hand in his.

We walk through the hallway as the Russian team leaves the ice and heads to the kiss and cry area. True to name, she's crying and they don't look like happy tears. The little girls from the local club in their best competition dresses finish gathering up the flowers and teddy bears from the ice.

Then I hear it. It starts low and then grows in volume and strength. The crowd has noticed Luc and I and they are cheering for us. They chant as one, *"U-S-A. U-S-A. U-S-A."*

I swallow back the lump in my throat.

"And now," *the announcer says.* "Representing the United States, Sophia Dubois and Luc Saucier!" *And the crowd goes wild as we step onto the ice.*

This. Is. It.

Luc and I step onto the ice hand in hand and make a lap around the ice before stopping in our opening position. I put one hand on my hip and lean forward to blow a kiss to the crowd to signal the start of our music.

Even though the short program is the technical program, Luc and I decided to have a little fun. This is the last Games for both of us, so we decided to do it up in style. With so much gossip circulating about me and my injuries last year, to Luc and his former partner, we thought a modern-day Bonnie and Clyde theme would be fantastic. So, we're skating to *It Ain't My Fault* by Brothers Osborne.

I let a huge smile spread across my face as the music picks up and we move across the ice in a footwork pattern before executing perfect side by side double axel, double lutz combos.

We skate around the backstop before he raises me up into one of my favorite lifts and then tosses me in the air before catching me and setting me back down.

Before we know it the routine is over, and the music has ended at the perfect timing. We're both a little out of breath but that's the adrenaline of the moment. Luc swings me around to drop into a graceful curtsy while he bows before the judges and then spins me around again to bow for the crowd. When I stand up he wraps his arms around me before taking my hand to lead me off the ice where Eugen is jumping up and down and clapping.

I have never, in all the years that he has coached me, seen this display of emotion.

We walk over to the kiss and cry to sit down—me in between Eugen and Luc. One of the local skating club girls hands me a teddy bear and some flowers.

"Thank you so much," I smile at her.

I take a deep breath. This is it. We skated the cleanest we ever have. I love this program, I choreographed this program and it's my baby. I hope that shows. But now it's out of our hands and it's up to the judges to decide.

"And now," *the announcer says, and I close my eyes.* "For technical . . . 10.0 . . . 10.0 . . . 9.5 . . ."

I gasp as the marks go on and on.

"And for artistic . . . 10.0 . . . 9.5 . . . 10.0 . . . 10.0." *This is insane. Our program was amazing, and all our hard work is finally paying off.* "The Americans take the lead."

Tears roll down my cheeks as Eugen and Luc hug me as we exit the kiss and cry. Kane is standing in the wings waiting for me.

"I knew you could do it, Tink."

He holds his arms wide for me and I happily step into them. Kane rubs my back while I smile and cry a little more before we head back to our staging area to take our skates off and head out.

Luc and I sign autographs at the exit before we head out to change and grab dinner. We won't do another press junket until after the final scores come down. If we place, Luc and I will have to meet with all of the big networks for interviews.

But right now, I'm going to enjoy the small victory, we won the first battle in the war and now it's time to celebrate just a tiny bit.

And just like that, Luc and I are in first place with Layla and Johan right behind us.

#Awkward

TEN

It's not what you think

"Sweet Kristi Yamaguchi's daisy dress," I whisper more to myself than anyone else as I stare at Layla's dead body. "You have got to be kidding me."

"This is not what you think," Luc says and there is a note of panic in his voice that makes me backup a step.

Last night, Kane, Luc, Eugen, and I had an early dinner at a lovely little bistro near the Olympic Village. While not traditional Korean fare, I enjoyed a lovely bowl of chicken alfredo and a Caesar salad. It was a nice treat after a wonderful competition.

We sat around the table and talked for over an hour while Kane and Eugen sipped glasses of dark red wine—Luc and I abstained as we are still competing—

before Luc excused himself for the night.

"I'm going to call it a night," Luc said as he rose from the table, tossing his napkin where his plate had been before kissing me on the cheek. "Great skate today."

"Don't go," I had whispered to his cheek.

"I have too," he had said. "She needs me."

"You're making a mistake, Luc."

"It's mine to make," he had said effectively ending the conversation. I let it go not wanting to ruin what we had accomplished today. "I'll see you at practice tomorrow."

"See you."

And that was that . . . until my phone rang this morning.

"Hello?" I had answered.

I was getting ready for our long program practice that was scheduled for later this morning. I had on a beautiful lavender practice dress and tights. My hair was pulled up into a clean ponytail at the back of my head and was dusting a soft pink blush onto my cheeks. I had set my makeup brush down to pick up my phone and slide my finger across the screen to unlock it.

"Sophie," Luc had said. "Something's wrong. I need you."

"Okay," I had responded as I would to anyone who was in need of help. This is what friends do. They help each other out. Maybe he needs cover while he does the walk of shame, or someone to look up how long you go with a priapism before calling for medical intervention. Maybe he even needs to tap into some of my thirty-two condoms per day savings which would make Kane really sad because he was really looking forward to those because they give athletes a variety and he had told me that the glow-in-the-dark ones are a real treat. I had never seen one before, so I have to take his word for it. "Where are you?"

"I'm a Layla and Johan's room," he had whispered into the phone and the anguish in his voice made a shiver dance up my spine. Verna would say that someone had stepped on my grave.

"I'll be right there," I had tried to reassure him.

"And Sophie?"

"Yes?"

"Come alone." With those parting words, he disconnected.

I slide my feet into my chucks and tucked my phone into my jacket pocket before quietly leaving the room. Natalie is playing her first game this morning at one of the hockey arenas that had been set up.

I didn't want to call attention to myself, so I had slipped a plain black fleece jacket on in exchange of my Team USA warm-up jacket before leaving. It was also warmer for my brisk walk through the Village lodgings.

When I get to their room, the door is ajar, so I knock softly before pushing it open to step inside. And instantly, I wish I hadn't when I take in the room.

Once again, the very foundation of my world had been rocked by violence.

A Thanksgiving Turkey. That's the first thought that pops into my head.

Layla is naked over a wingback chair. Her beautiful body is trussed up like a Thanksgiving turkey. Rough ropes are intricately tied all around her body and I can't help but stare.

I've never seen anything like it before. It's almost beautiful minus the fact that it's what obviously killed her. It doesn't take a forensic specialist to see the rope knotted around her neck. Her eyes are wide, and her face is blue. I have no idea how long she's been here like this and only one thought rolls through my head and I admit that it's a little bit selfish. Luc Saucier has killed his lover, one of our toughest competitors, and now I'm not going to get a chance at Olympic style redemption.

"Sweet Kristi Yamaguchi's daisy dress," I whisper more to myself than anyone else as I stare at Layla's dead body. "You have got to be kidding me."

"This is not what you think," Luc says and there is a note of panic in his voice that makes me backup a step.

"Really?" I ask as my anger rises up to the surface. What kind of bubble headed moron does he think I am? I wasn't born yesterday. "Because it looks to me like you are standing over the dead body of our competitor."

"Okay," Luc says hesitantly as he holds his hands up towards me as if he's gentling a spooked horse. And that's exactly what I am—*spooked*. "It is what it looks like."

"Darn it, Luc!" I snap. "How could you?"

"What?" he says surprised. "You can't possibly think that I did this?"

"Well, I don't really know what to think right now, now do I?" I bite back. "Last time I saw you, you were leaving to meet her for a-a-a rendezvous!" I fling out my arm to indicate Layla's dead body as the her he was leaving to meet.

"Sophie, please," he pleads. "You've got to believe me."

"This looks bad, Luc," I tell him. "Really, really bad."

"I know." He lets out a frustrated sigh and pushes a hand through his thick hair. "I don't know what to do but I didn't do this."

Luc and I stand there, facing each other off, with Layla's body sprawled over a chair between us. I'm not sure which is more disconcerting, the ropes tied around her nude body or the ones tied around her neck.

"Please don't run from me. I'm not going to hurt you." He looks sad, stricken even. I don't know how much Luc had come to care for Layla or if she was just a fling, but the idea of her hurt—or me afraid of him—has him shaken.

"I'm not going to lie, Luc, this scares me," I admit.

"I know. Me too," he whispers into the room.

He sighs again and pulls his hand through his hair. The silence between us speaks volumes. This was supposed to be my second chance at the Games. My last one as a singles competitor was taken from me by my stepmonster and her evil henchman when they broke my leg. So, when the opportunity to replace half of a pairs team came up, I jumped on it. Now, it seems like I should have paid more attention to the fine print. You'd think by now I would have learned that life always hands an opportunity with a catch, and addendum that should be heeded like a warning because now I'm in one heck of a pickle.

"You have to believe me," he pleads with those big, brown puppy dog eyes, the ones that have probably gotten him out of more scrapes than he deserves. Let's just hope that this is one of them.

I let out a sigh and admit, "I do."

"Thank fuck," Luc blurts out. "But what are we going to do now?"

I wish like heck that I knew myself. This is more than a little complication.

"I don't know." What I do know is that my mostly on-again boyfriend is not going to be thrilled when he hears what happened.

Kane is going to be so mad—he's going to be pissed—*excuse my French.*

I let out a sigh and pull my phone from my pocket

before changing my answer to one that I know Luc is absolutely going to hate. "We have to call Kane."

"No!" he practically shouts.

"If you didn't do this, we need help because right now, you look guilty as sin," I tell him as I start to dial Kane's number.

"I know, but anyone but him," Luc says.

"No, especially him," I say giving him my serious business face. "What you need is the best and that's Kane."

"Fucking Green," he groans. "Fine. Call him."

I finish dialing his number, it only rings twice before he answers.

"What's up, Tink? Aren't you supposed to be at practice?" Kane asks me.

"Yeah," I answer. "About that . . ."

"Tink?"

"I need your help, Kane," I whisper into the phone letting him hear how scared I really am before I tell him where I am. I don't give him any more details. I just tell Kane that I need him and where I am and he answers me in the very best of ways.

"I'm on my way."

ELEVEN

Our closet crapping Cujo

"**N**o. Fucking. Way," Kane seethes from the doorway.

I'll admit that this is probably my fault. I should have prepared him better for seeing Layla trussed up like a Christmas goose, but the whole morning has been jarring. I'm not in possession of all of my faculties, I guess. It's been a trying week.

My bad.

"Kane—" I start.

"No, Sophia," he cuts me off.

"But Ka—"

"Not a chance, sweetheart," he clips out. "I need a minute to cool down here."

"Kane!" I shout. "Would you just let me talk, please?"

"No!" Kane snaps at me. "Because you are just going to ask me to help Saucier who is obviously guilty of fucking murder." I watch Luc flinch as Kane delivers his killing blow to a man who has become a friend to me even if he has behaved ike an ass this past week.

"He didn't do it, Kane," I whisper.

"You don't know that," he argues. "You know that they were having an affair and so does everyone else."

"I know that," I explain to Kane while poor Luc looks on. "But he didn't do it."

"Hell, even her husband knew he was banging her," Kane bites out.

"But he didn't do it and it you think about it for a moment, you would admit that you don't think he did it either," I say softly.

"This looks really bad, Tink." Kane lets out a weary sigh before pushing his hand through his hair.

"I know." I wrap my arms around his waist and lay my head on his chest. I take in a deep breath and let it out when Kane closes his arms around me.

"He's a menace," he says softly.

"Nah," I tell him. "He's more like the puppy that craps in your closet than Cujo the killer dog that is going to rip your face off in your sleep and enjoy it."

"Probably," Kane agrees with me on a sigh.

"I'm right here, guys," Luc says from the other side of the room.

"We know," Kane tells him on a smirk.

"And we're going to help you," I add supportively.

"Apparently." Kane rolls his eyes. "And I like your use of the royal 'we', babe."

"Good," I say on a smirk. "Get used to it."

Kane pulls out his phone and calls the police. "Yes, I'd like to report a crime in the Olympic Village . . . I'm sure there *is* a fair amount of crime during the Games," he says. "But not like *this* . . . Lady, I'm sure . . . have you ever seen a dead body trussed up like a Christmas Goose? . . . That's what I thought . . . We'll be waiting. Thank you."

"That . . . umm . . . sounded like it went well," I tell him. Kane side eyes me with that look that he gets when he is immensely frustrated with me. I move to take a step back, but he grabs me by the jacket and hauls me back into his arms. Darn loose material that's easy to grab.

"It did not think it went well," Kane disagrees. "This is going to be a nightmare."

"I'm sorry," I say softly.

Kane lets out a breath. "The police will be here soon," Kane explains. "As soon as the police question you, if you are released, you need to contact the U. S. and Canadian Consulates for assistance."

"What if they don't release me?" Luc asks. His voice is both hoarse and quiet from being unused but I can still hear the fear that lies beneath the surface of his words and by the set to Kane's shoulders and the look on his face, he hears it too.

"Then definitely contact the consulates," he says. "I don't know how their government works here so we have to proceed with caution."

"Should we hide him?" I ask.

"No!" they both snap at me.

"I won't hide," Luc says. "I didn't do anything wrong."

"I didn't say that you did," I say softly trying to smooth over his hurt feelings.

"He has to tell the truth here. I'm talking full transparency so that we can get to the bottom of this," Kane adds.

"What if we never find out who did it?" Luc asks.

"Don't worry, we will," Kane says with more confidence than I currently feel.

I want to pace. Whenever I'm under a certain level of stress—much like right now—I feel restless and need to move my body. I need to run but that is the last thing I should do. Luc needs me right now and as angry as I was with him for making us look bad while he was galivanting around the Olympic Village with Layla, I will not leave him here to defend himself. Right now, I am not entirely sure that he could so the last thing I need to do is make Luc look guilty by distancing myself from him or running away even though that's what my gut is telling me to do.

I'm not afraid of him, but the situation. I barely survived my last head to head with a murderer. I had a level of blind confidence born of naivete going into my search for Vadim's killer a year ago. But now, I'm not so sure. I feel weary and frightened. I learned some hard lessons then and the number one hard truth I had

had to swallow was that you can't trust everyone you know. That sometimes the people you should trust are the people you know that you shouldn't and that those who should protect you above all else would sooner feed you to the wolves than not.

"Don't touch anything," Kane says when I move a step over.

"I won't," I whisper softly.

"Did you touch anything before I got here?" Kane asks.

"No," I answer him honestly.

"Did you?" he asks Luc who swallows audibly.

"I had to see if she was alive," he rasps before further breaking my heart. "I-I had wanted to save her."

"Okay," Kane says, and I can practically hear the wheels turning in his head. I see his eyes ping around the room at large with a purpose. "Did you touch the ropes?"

"No."

"Good," Kane says. "What did you touch?"

"Just her wrist," Luc says.

"Nothing else?" Kane presses on.

"No," Luc answers and his body language looks to me as though he is telling the truth and I believe in that even though my instincts have lead me astray in the past.

"Don't lie to me," Kane warns. "If I am going to help you I need to know everything."

"I promise that's everything," Luc says before he

begins explaining to us what happened this morning. "Sophie and I had an official practice set for late morning, but I received a text from Layla early this morning that she wanted to see me here."

"Do you still have the message on your phone?" Kane asks.

"Yes," Luc answers.

"Show me," Kane demands softly before Luc slides his finger across the screen to unlock his phone. He brings up his text message app and shows Kane and I the message. "Don't touch anything but I don't see a phone anywhere in here."

"I didn't either," Luc agrees.

"I would bet the killer sent you that message to try and make you look guilty," Kane says on a grimace. "And I would bet someone killed her late last night by the looks of things. What happened next?"

"I got ready for practice early thinking I would stop over here on my way to the bus pickup to make sure she was alright," Luc explains.

"Why would you think anything would be amiss with Layla?" Kane asks.

"Everyone knew that their marriage was over but Johan," Luc explains. "She was worried that he would be angry when they didn't out rank Sophia and I after the short program."

"Does Johan get angry often?" Kane asked.

"Not that I have seen with my own eyes, but there were rumors."

"Did Layla ever repeat these rumors to you?" Kane asks.

"Yes."

Kane sighs. Of course, she did. Layla may God rest her soul, was a manipulative bitch. I have no doubt in my mind that she told Luc a whole lot of things to make him feel sorry for her and look where it got him now?

"And what happened when you got here?" Kane asks.

"The door wasn't closed all the way," Luc describes the scene. "I thought that was weird, but Johan is often forgetful if he's taken his sleeping medication the night before. I went to knock on the door and it swung open."

"And then what?" Kane asks, and I feel like I am hanging on their every word.

"I saw her, Layla, tied up around the chair. I though—" he cuts his speech off and swallows before pressing on. "I had thought that she was alive, and I could save her."

"Luc," I whisper.

"But I couldn't," he finishes softly.

"Did Layla often engage in this kind of sexual play?" Kane asks.

"Sexual?" I repeat. Surely, this was some kind of attack, not love play. Who would want to be tied up and brutalized like that? What Luc does not do is answer.

"Saucier?" Kane calls out. "I asked if Layla engaged in this kind of sexual play often?"

"Yes," he whispers.

"Always or sometimes?"

"Always."

"Is there anything else?" Kane asks. "I don't want any surprises."

"That's it," Luc swears. "I promise."

"Okay," Kane agrees.

"Why are you helping me?" Luc asks after a moment.

"Because Sophie asked me to," Kane answers. "And because it's the right thing to do." Just like that, I knew without a doubt that I was right all along to put my trust in Kane Green. I never should have shut him out while I trained for this competition. I should have talked to him months ago so that we could share our fears and our worries and get over them together. I wasted so much time with him and for that, I am truly sorry. I can't go back in time and fix it, I can only go forward.

Who would have thought that Kane Fucking Green would be it for me?

"Thank you."

"Don't thank me yet," Kane says before the police sirens become loud enough to hear.

The police storm in with guns drawn and ask questions later. As it turns out, we didn't have to worry about Luc being taken into custody because we were all taken into custody until we could be interviewed one by one.

I just hope that I can clear all this up before my dad gets wind of the situation back in the states.

And if you believe that's possible too, I've got some ocean front property in Arizona . . .

TWELVE

Shit in one hand and wish in the other

I never should have wasted the breath to wish and hope that my dad wouldn't find out what a mess we were in here in Korea. It's like Verna always says, "You can shit in one hand and wish in the other and see which one fills up faster." As crude as it is, she's not wrong. One day I will learn to stop wishing and hoping.

When the local police showed up Kane, Luc, and I were all loaded in separate official vehicles and spirited away into the bowels of the local police station. I can't speak for Kane and Luc, but I was deposited into a small, windowless room that contained a beat-up metal table with one battered metal chair on either side.

"Sit down," the officer had barked in heavily accented English.

So, I did what I was told, and I sat down on one

side of the table. While the officer left the room. The substantial door shutting behind him with a thud.

I let out a resigned sigh. There is literally nothing I can do to change my current situation and I find that you catch more flies with honey than you do with vinegar, so I sit there with my arms folded on top of the table.

I focus on my breathing, making a conscious effort to steady it. I count out each long breath in and each breath out. I long ago learned that when life was raining down on me and everything was out of my control, that I could control myself. That I could control my reaction to the world around me. After that, I started studying yoga and meditation. Not just chili Tuesday yoga when I could with my friends back home, but advanced yoga. I like being able to clear my concentration and force myself to be calm.

So that's exactly what I do.

I have no idea how long I had sat there, but it was long enough that my muscles feel stiff from being unused for a lengthy period of time. My backside is numb and stings at the same time.

The door pushes open.

"Excuse me, Miss Dubois," the officer says apologetically. "You should have told us who you were so that we could show you the appropriate deference."

"There is nothing to forgive," I tell him on my sweetest smile. "You were only doing your job and it is my duty as the partner of a law enforcement officer back in the United States that I aid you in any way I can so that we may find justice for poor Layla."

He seems to like my theory and smiles broadly at me. "You are most kind, Miss Dubois."

"Thank you so much," I tell him sweetly.

"You are free to go," he says on a deep bow.

"Thank you, again," I tell him. "And my friends? The men that I came here with?"

"They are still being questioned," he answers me with a frown marring his face. Well that does not bode well for Kane and Luc. If Kane does not get out of here soon he is going to be absolutely furious—with me and everyone else involved.

"Do I still need to be questioned?" I ask the officer. I have no issue being questioned and I want to get to the bottom of things before it's too late.

"No, Miss Dubois," he says. "We have been notified of your diplomatic immunity."

Huh, I had forgotten about that little gem. Good to know. Although it's not going to help me right now, it exists for a reason and I need to toe the line here. Right now, I need to be on my best behavior so that I can find out as much information as I can.

"Thank you," I tell him again as I push to stand up from my chair.

I follow him out into the lobby where several Secret Service Agents are waiting to spirit me away. And just like Dorothy Hamill's famous pixie cut, this can, unfortunately, only mean one thing.

My dad is here.

And I am so screwed.

"Everything is all set, Miss Dubois," one of the men in black says to me. He's clearly the leader here and I have no desire to make trouble for him or anyone else. It kind of takes me back to my time in Paris where Kane was my number one agent. I squint my eyes as I try and remember that time more clearly and if I have ever seen this man before or if he's new to my Dad's detail.

"Thank you," I tell him.

The secret service agents that my dad sent to collect me circle their wagons around me and I look back to the officer that had walked me out. I spy him sneaking back out. I don't blame him, not really, I would sneak out too if I wasn't used to this kind of display of power and prestige. I call out to him just as he pulls open the door.

"Please do keep an eye out for the gentlemen that I can with," I plead my case for help. "And if you would be so kind as to tell Detective Green that my father has sent for me I would really appreciate it. He worries so."

"Detective Green has been notified that your custody has been transferred to our care," the agent informs me.

"Oh dear," I say more to myself than anyone else.

"You got that right," the agent says. "To say that your boyfriend was upset would be an understatement."

"Yikes."

"That too," the agent says. "He threw a chair at me and said that he'd gut me like a fish if anything happens to you before he could get to you."

"Yep," I agree with a broad smile. "That sounds like Kane."

The officer looks a little frightened and I probably would too if I didn't think Kane was the best thing since the triple axel. But what can I say? I'm a woman in love. But that also answers my question, he's clearly not familiar with all that is Kane Fucking Green.

"Do hurry to clear Detective Green," I say one last time before the officer scurries back through the door. The look on his face says that we're all absolutely bonkers and, truth be told, we probably are. It can't be helped and there's no sense dwelling on it, so . . .

"We should go, ma'am. The Senator is waiting," the lead agent says to me before guiding me to the door.

Famous last words.

The men in black surround me as they walk me out to a waiting town car. One of the others gets behind the wheel as they open the rear door for me and I slide all the way in per their protocol. One slides in beside me and the last one climbs into the front passenger seat. I am surrounded, and I can't help but feel a little like a prisoner being escorted to death row. I didn't even get my final meal! As if on cue, my stomach growls. Our official practice has long since come and gone. So had lunch time and I am starving.

"I'm sure we can get you something to eat while you meet with the Senator," the agent next to me says.

"That would be lovely," I say on a bright smile. "Thank you."

He seems to be a little startled, by what, I am not totally sure, and he shakes his head like an etch-a-sketch to clear it before facing forward again. Clearly, he's not looking to be best buddies and while I would like to have an actual friend among my father's camp, that is probably not the best course of action. Kane would probably lose his mind if I was friends with one of the studly, young agents.

I let out a sigh as we pull into the back entrance of a prestigious hotel near the Olympic Village. These rooms have been sold out for over two years. Although, it would stand to reason that my dad had one booked for him since I was slated to be here before my injury. Not that he's ever been to one of my competitions, but I guess it doesn't look too good for a Presidential hopeful to be absent from their daughter's support team at the freaking Olympics.

The men in black assigned to me for however long now that I have proved that I'm incapable of staying out of trouble file out of the car, except for the driver, and open the door for me before surrounding me. We enter through a back entrance of the hotel. My dad clearly does not want my face splashed across the media any more than it already has been.

We ride the service and freight elevator up to the

penthouse suite and I'm not even surprised. But it's not my dad that I see when the steel doors slide open on a ding, but his Majordomo.

"Somebody's in trouble," she sing songs as we file off of the elevator.

"I hate to break it to you," I say on a wink with the express purpose of riling her up. "But this isn't the first time and it's not going to be the last."

"Oh, we'll just see about that," she says. "Stay in the living room. I'll tell the Senator that you're here now."

I sit down on the sofa and cross my legs while thinking that I'd really love a pizza right about now and then feeling sad because I'm not allowed to eat pizza while I'm training. My body is a temple and all that jazz. I'll be lucky to get grilled chicken and vegetables for dinner tonight. Maybe even a glass of milk. Living large.

"Really, Sophia," my dad snaps as he enters the room and I jump up. He walks over and hugs me tightly for just a second before releasing me and I flop back down into my seat almost believing that the whole thing had only happened in my imagination.

"Hi, Dad," I say softly.

He sighs. "What part of being on your best behavior didn't you understand?"

"Luc didn't murder anyone," I explain. "He's being set up and I can't just sit back and let him take the fall."

"I know," he says sounding older than he ever has before.

"You do?" I ask.

"When I heard that he was being investigated for murder I knew that you would be in the thick of it," my dad explains. "Especially after what happened last year."

I'm actually surprised that he brought that up. Usually, Dad doesn't want to talk about the events that led to my almost murder and definite disqualification last year. If anything, he wants to pretend like the whole thing never happened.

"I'm sorry," I say honestly. I am, really. I don't want to cause trouble for my dad. We don't always see eye to eye on everything—or well, anything—but that doesn't mean that I don't love him. I do. "I don't mean to cause you trouble."

"Now, I find that hard to believe," he says sounding like he's still a little angry.

"Really," I explain. "I don't do it on purpose. It just kind of happens."

"So, you just 'kind of' got married after telling me that you weren't in a hurry to marry anyone," he says casually, and I have to wonder if I heard him right or if maybe I have developed some kind of split personality disorder. Or is it some kind of dissociative disorder? I'm not really sure. I guess I should do a little research if I have up and gone crazy overnight.

Can you lose all of your faculties overnight?

Again, I'm not sure.

"Excuse me?" I ask seriously for clarification.

"I think you heard me," my dad says.

"I don't think I did or else I might be losing my mind because it sounded like you said that I got married when I told you that I wasn't going to marry anyone anytime soon," I explain. I'm so confused. I'm pretty sure there was no white dress befitting of a princess, no priest, no flowers . . . but there were the flowers that Kane bought me outside of his friends' tea house.

"You heard right," he practically growls.

"I'm pretty sure that I would know if I got married—" I start to say.

"Would you?" my dad asks.

"Of course—" and then I remember the tea house and Kane's friends that didn't speak any English but he managed to learn perfect Korean in that time. *I just knew that there was something off that night.*

I smell a rat and his name is Kane Fucking Green. I can't believe he tricked me into marrying him. Instead of just freaking asking. I rake my hands through my hair making my ponytail look ridiculous.

"Holy Sonja Henie, I got married," I whisper.

THIRTEEN

Dildos and Public Relations

"Sophia—" my dad starts but I hold up my hand to silence him. I need a second to process everything right now.

I married Kane Fucking Green.

And I didn't even know it!

There is so much ridiculousness that is happening right now that I can't even comprehend it. How could he? I'm so hurt and so mad right now. He should have asked me in some ridiculously romantic fashion with flowers, candles, and a lot of sex—although, if I'm being honest with myself we did have the sex part—but still . . .

"Sophia are you listening to me?" my dad says.

"Don't even start," I tell him honestly. I don't think I can handle much more heaped on top of me.

"We have to get this annulled," Majordomo says. "Now."

"You will do no such thing," I snap. And it would seem that I have hit my breaking point.

"Be reasonable here," my dad says. "You're not thinking clearly, Sophia." Or really, I've finally seen everything clearly. What Kane did wasn't right, but it wasn't wrong either.

We belong together.

"No, you're not listening," I tell them. I make them look me in the eye so that they can see how very serious I am. "Kane is mine to deal with and you will leave my marriage alone."

"Here, here!" The Dames shout from the doorway.

"How did you all get in here?" Dad's Majordomo demands.

"I let them in," the agent that sat with me in the car says before he winks at me.

"Looks like we just made it here in the nick time," Verna says.

"I hardly think you have a place here," my dad says to one of my most favorite people in the world. She's like the Grandmother that I never got to know.

"Hey!" I say.

"Oh, stuff it you pompous windbag," Marla cackles.

"Looks like you're still being an enormous bag of dicks, Senator," Verna replies as she rolls her eyes.

"Let's go, ladies," I tell them. "We have better places to be."

"We will talk about this later, daughter," my dad

says to me as I stand to leave.

"Oh, I'm sure that we will," I tell him. "Just leave my marriage alone. There is a lot that I can forgive, but not that."

"I think we need lunch," Shelby chimes in—God bless her. "Where should we go?"

"I hear there's a great tavern around the corner," I answer her question.

"Fantastic!" she cheers. "Let's do it!"

"I'm here for that!" Daisy cheers and the new girl, Alyssa, laughs. She's quiet and I haven't had much time to get to know her, but I like her.

We walk out the front door of the hotel and into the sunshine—and paparazzi flashbulbs.

"What were you doing in the hotel, Sophie?" one of them calls out to me. I smile my best daughter of a politician smile and answer.

"Just visiting." I wink at them. "Have a good day!"

We walk around the corner to the tavern and as soon as we walk in the door it takes me a moment to clear my eyes against the haze of smoke and dim lighting. I spot Johan the second we walk in cozied up with one of the French ice dancers looking anything like a man mourning the murder of his wife.

"Isn't that the dude whose wife just bought it?" Daisy asks in a stage whisper.

"Yeah," I say softly. "That's him."

"Suddenly, I'm not so hungry," Verna says, and I can't help but feel the same way.

"Hey, baby," I overhear him say. "I'm going to get another drink from the bar. Need another?"

"Yeah," she breathes out in a kind of—and I really hate to say it because I am really uncomfortable speaking ill of people—a slutty voice.

"Be right back," he says.

He stiffens his back when he sees us in the doorway of the tavern as he makes his way to the bar. He pauses only for a second on his way to lock eyes with me.

"You have some nerve coming here, Dubois," he snarls at me and I'm not going to lie, I'm a little surprised to hear how angry he is with me.

"I don't know what you're talking about," I say honestly. And I don't. Whatever could his beef be with me?

"Your partner fucked my wife," he says, his voice rising in volume. "And then he killed her."

"Luc didn't kill her," I shout back.

"How can you even say that?" Johan says. He's clearly warming up to his cause. "You saw him yourself standing over her body."

Now, how would he know that? I narrow my eyes at him and Johan has the nerve to wink at me when no one was looking. He knows, he freaking knows that I saw them and he's using it to make Luc look guilty, but why?

"Can't deny it, can you?" he asks. When I don't answer him, he says, "That's what I thought."

So much for due process. It looks like Luc is being tried in the court of public opinion.

"Now that's a bigger dildo than the one in my pocketbook," Verna says louder than I think anyone in this bar is comfortable with.

"Granny," Shelby admonishes her grandmother but the way that she's biting her lip to quell her laughter speaks volumes. She's not really mad to find out her grandmother and her friend had brought a bevy of fake penises and marital aids to a foreign country. Truth be told, I didn't really expect her to be. If anything, Shelby is an enabler to Verna's hijinks and they wouldn't have it any other way. I envy their relationship.

"Of course, I did," Verna says on a laugh. "You never know when Big Thunder will come in handy and you know poor Marla couldn't bring the eagle with her."

"Thank Christ," Shelby mumbles.

"What was that, dear?" Verna asks Shelby. "I could have sworn I heard you take the Lord's name in vain but that couldn't be true now could it?"

"Of course not." Shelby winks at me.

"That's what I thought," Verna says before turning her attention to me. "My Shelby is a good girl."

I just smile at her and nod. Shelby is a wonderful woman and one that I am lucky to call a friend, but she is not a *good girl*. Shelby takes after Verna more than either of her parents. She's going to be hell on wheels when she's eighty, by her own admission.

FOURTEEN

The calm before the storm A.K.A Kane is a
dead man

"There you are, Sophie," Kane says as he busts through the front door of the tavern. "I have been looking for you all over."

I didn't have the time since my dad spilled the beans about Kane tricking me into marrying him to fantasize about how I would confront him when I finally saw him again, what I would say to him. I think that's a good thing because I haven't had the opportunity to let my feelings fester. Unfortunately, it means that I am flustered when he walks through the door.

"Soph," he says as he snaps his fingers in my face. "You in there, babe?"

"When were you going to tell me?" I ask, the words just blurting out of my mouth like diarrhea.

"Uhh . . ." he says, and I look at him, I really look at Kane, and see that he looks nervous.

"Were you going to tell me?" I ask softly. "Or were you just going to keep it from me forever.?"

"I was going to tell you eventually," Kane admits.

I hear a "Harrumph" come from over my shoulder. It seems somehow the grannies got popcorn and they seem pretty interested in the Sophie and Kane show. If it was anyone else I would be really upset, but these ladies have a vested interest in our lives. They're involved, and they care.

"Eventually isn't good enough, Kane," I tell him.

"I was just so afraid I would lose you.," Kane admits. He swallows audibly.

"I'm not sure that you haven't," I snap, and I instantly regret the angry words that I let fly from my mouth.

"Sophie, you know that's not true," Kane says with a confidence that resonates through me.

"I don't have any idea what the truth is, now do I, Kane?" Apparently, I'm not done being angry with Kane. Which is pretty ironic since I basically told my dad and his henchwoman that if they had my marriage annulled, I would never speak to them again. I let out a sigh. I really need to get my head on straight.

So, I do the only thing that I can think of. I turn on my heel and walk out the door.

"Wait!" Kane shouts from somewhere behind me. "Sophie, wait."

He must have followed me outside and I have to admit that I'm glad he came after me. There was a small part of me that wasn't so sure that he would after I threw it in his face that I didn't want him anymore.

I stop walking and turn around in time to see Kane jog up to me. He pulls me into his arms and holds me tight for a while before he speaks. I wrap my arms around him and just hold on. There are so many things that have gone so very wrong in the last twenty-four hours that I just need to hold on. I need to hold on to Kane, to us, to whatever we have left that I haven't ruined with my anger.

"I'm so sorry, Tink," he whispers in my ear. "I was just so scared that I would lose you to Saucier or one of your daddy's bevy of congressmen he seems to have waiting in the wings or someone else. I never should have doubted your feelings for me. Please forgive me. I'm just so damn sorry, Tink."

"I'm sorry too, Kane," I tell him. "I shouldn't have been so cruel. I was mad, and I took it out on you and I shouldn't have."

"It's all over now," he says.

"Uhh . . ." I mumble as I look up into his beautiful blue eyes, eyes that lied to me but for valid reasons that I can understand. I no longer feel insecure where I stand with Kane because we were both feeling the same way and wanting to be tied to each other in the most permanent way and no we are. We could have gone about it differently, and we both know that we shold have, but we are here now and there is no going back. Not for me and definitely, not for Kane either.

We're in this together.

"Well, we do still have to find out who killed Saucier's married lover," he says as if it's no big deal.

"There is that," I agree.

"Maybe we should get out of here," he says to me. "What do you say?"

"I say lead the way."

Kane takes me by the hand and leads me to another hotel about a block away. He breaks into a little bit of a jog and I hear that old Tiffany song playing in my head. With everything going on, our surprise marriage—well, it was a surprise for me, not for Kane—and Luc being blamed for Layla's murder. I'm still not completely over the fact that Layla preferred a certain . . . um . . . style in the bedroom. I know that I'm not that experienced in that arena, but still. I have a lot of questions and I don't know who to ask.

I look to Kane as we make our way towards his hotel and wonder if maybe my husband is the guy to ask after all. But also, I know that he is more experienced than me by a boat load. He was dating another woman when we met after all. Do I want to know about his experiences with other women? Does it even matter now that we're married? Part of me thinks that if he was so afraid to lose me that he tricked me into marrying him, maybe I have nothing to worry about. Maybe none of those women in the past matter to Kane anymore or at all.

The front of the hotel is littered with paparazzi

when we make it there. Too bad we were so wrapped up in this intimate moment together that we didn't notice them until it was too late.

"Fuck!" Kane bites out. "I should have taken you around the back."

I shrug my shoulders. "It probably wouldn't have done any good. Someone else is probably back there anyways."

"Sophie! Sophie!" they call out my name.

"It is true that you secretly got married while here in Korea?" one of them asks me.

"Well now," I answer on my winning smile. "It's not a secret if you know about it, is it?"

They all laugh.

"It is true that your husband tricked you into marrying him?" someone asks.

"Of course not," I lie to them. "Kane is the hero here. Remember, he's saved my life more than once."

"It was rumored that you were being courted by a congressman with close ties to your father, what do you say to that?"

"Hogwash!" I laugh. "You can line your bird cages with that one, guys. I have been in love with Kane Green ever since I met him in Paris two years ago. Now if you'll excuse us . . ."

I trudge forward while pulling Kane behind me by the hand before stopping at the elevator to push the call button. I look back over my shoulder and smile and wave.

"Smile," I whisper to Kane and he looks over my shoulder and scowls. "I said smile."

He looks to me before pasting a knowing smirk on his face. Darn it, but that smirk does things to me. And double darn it if he doesn't know it, which of course, Kane Fucking Green does.

"Act like you're madly in love with me," I whisper.

Kane pulls me into his arms and leans down planting the whopper of all kisses on me. I whimper a little and he uses that opportunity to lick into my mouth and deepen the kiss. It's something out of a movie. So tender and sexy at the same time. When he pulls back I drag as much air into my lungs as I possibly can while Kane rocks my world in another way.

"Baby, I don't have to act like I'm madly in love with you because I already am," he says as if he was telling me that the Queen is British.

"What?" I ask breathlessly just as the elevator doors open on a ding.

He pulls me into the elevator with one more casual wave to the photographers just outside the glass front doors of the hotel. The steel doors slide closed and Kane reaches over to push the button for his floor, but he does not let go of me to do it.

"Was it true what you said out there or just bullshit for the paps?" he asks, his voice husky in my ear.

"What was bullsh—?" I just barely stop myself from saying the words that he uses. I'm so lost in his baby blue eyes. You would think that by now I would be immune to his charms but all it takes is his eyes on mine and I'm gone.

"What you said about being in love with me since we met in Paris?"

I feel the heat of my self-consciousness creep up my neck and over my cheeks as they scald red with my embarrassment. Even though we're married now, there is still a level of vulnerability that I'm not comfortable with yet. Could I lay myself bare for him? Can I tell Kane the truth of how long I've felt for him? How deep his betrayal in France had cut me?

All it takes is one more look at Kane to know that he would slay all my dragons for me and lay the world at my feet if only I let him. So, I answer him the only way that I can—honestly.

"It's the truth," I whisper and look quickly away. I'm so nervous that I can't seem to muster my voice to a higher volume. Is it hot in here? Suddenly, this elevator is on fire.

The elevator dings to tell us that we have arrived at the floor.

"Thank fuck," Kane barks out and it breaks me free from my thoughts.

"What?" I ask as he ushers me off of the elevator and leads me down the hall to stop in front of a door. He reaches into his pocket and pulls out a key card.

"Thank fuck we're here because now I have to fuck you," he says as he slides the key card into the lock and pushes the door open.

"What?" I ask again as the door slams closed and Kane backs me up against it, cornering me.

"Baby, with what you gave me out on the street and again in the elevator," he tells me as he trails his fingertip over my brow and down my cheek. "I have to be inside you."

"Okay," I whisper, and he smiles that winning smile.

"Okay," he repeats. "Now, do you want me to fuck you or do you want to sit on my face first?"

My cheeks burn again and Kane chuckles. When he sees it, he traces the color that spreads across the apples of my cheeks. And I whisper my answer.

"What was that?" he leans in with a wicked smile playing on his lips. That devil knows exactly what I said and he's not going to let me get off easy—literally. "I didn't quite hear you."

"I said I want to sit on your face," I whisper.

"Good choice, Tink," he practically growls as he pulls my fleece jacket over my head and tosses it to the floor. "I love to eat your pussy."

"Kane!" I gasp as he pushes my warm-up pants down my legs. I have to step out of my chucks as he pulls the legs of my pants over my feet.

"Sweetest pussy I've ever tasted," he rumbles as he stands back up.

"Shh!" I try and cove his mouth, but he just laughs. "Someone might hear you."

"Then they will know that I'm crazy for you," he

says as he leans back to look at me. "Fuck if I know why these little skating dresses of yours turn me on so bad but they do."

Kane slides his fingers into the neckline of my navy-blue velvet practice dress and pushes it down past my breasts. The shoulders pin my arms to my sides and bares me for him to see.

He cups my breast in his calloused hand and circles my nipple with his thumb. It tightens under his touch and I arch into him ever so slightly.

Kane slides his other hand up from my waist to cup my other breast the same way he had the first as he kisses me behind my ear. There is something about that spot that makes all thought leave my brain. I don't know what it is about it, but ever since Kane found it he exploits its power mercilessly.

He licks, nips, and kisses his way down the side of my neck and even further down until he opens his mouth over my nipple and draws it in deep. I moan and wiggle a little. I need more and at this point I would to anything to get it. Kane bites down on my nipple in warning and I let out a little yelp.

Kane lets my nipple go with a pop before pushing my dress down my body the rest of the way. He drops down to kneel in front of me as he rolls my tights down with my dress and lets his hands slide down each leg as he helps me to step free of them, one by one.

"Knowing that you're completely naked under these little dresses does something to me, Tink," Kane says as he presses his palm to the fly of his jeans.

I reach down and grab his polo shirt in my hands and slowly draw it up over his head. Kane hasn't played professional hockey in years, but you would never know it looking at his toned body. Each muscle looks like it was chiseled from granite and a few tattoos mark the skin of his torso from his wilder days. I bit my lip as I look at him because he does things to me too.

Slowly, ever so slowly, Kane raises one of my legs up and places a gentle kiss on my inner thigh before draping my leg over his shoulder. He grips my backside in his strong hands and lifts me up against the hotel room door as he shifts me to drop my other leg over his shoulder.

"You're so beautiful," Kane says just before he licks up my seam. "And so very sweet."

"Kane," I gasp as I arch against his mouth.

He circles the tip of his tongue around my clit and I cry out as I claw at his hair. Kane wears it just long enough on top that I have something to hold on to and I love to pull it just a little bit.

Kane slides a finger deep inside me and I gasp as he pumps his finger in and out as he circles my clit with his tongue. It's too much and at the same time not enough. Kane is driving me crazy. He burns me up from the inside out.

"Kane," I beg.

He rolls my clit into his mouth and sucks deep as

he adds a second finger. It's just what I need to push me over the edge and I come on a gasp.

Kane pushes up from the floor with my legs still wrapped around his neck and his mouth on my center. I let out an undignified squeak for someone who gets thrown in the air on the ice all the time when he does.

He kneels down on the bed before leaning forward to drop me to my back and I bounce once . . . twice . . . before Kane leans over and takes my mouth in a bruising kiss of teeth and tongue. He runs his cock up and down through my slit coating himself with my arousal.

"I love how wet you are for me," he growls as he slides in deep in one thrust.

"Yes." I put my hands to his shoulders as Kane grips my legs behind my knees and pushes them up my chest. I adjust to the new position with ease and he slides in and out.

"So fucking bendy," Kane groans as he leans back to watch as his cock glides in and out of my body. "It's so fucking sexy."

"Yes," I pant. I can't help but agree as I watch my husband watching where his body joins mine.

Kane pushes up and out on my legs so that his hands hold me in an open straddle position while he pumps in and out of my body, faster and faster.

"Kane," I beg. "Harder. I need you harder."

He drives in and out of my body and I clench around him. The position not only leaves me totally open to him but also forces him deeper than ever.

"Kane," I cry out as he pumps even harder. "Baby, I need to come.

"Say it," he demands. "Give me what you gave me earlier and I will."

"I love you!" As soon as I say the words, Kane drops my legs and I curl them up around his hips while he reaches between us to stroke my clit. I'm so close that it won't take much.

"I love you too, Tink," he growls against my mouth as he thrusts harder and harder, his movements becoming more and more wild by the second.

I arch my head back against the bed and scream as I come.

Kane grips my hips in his hands a thrust hard once, twice, before planting deep inside and joining me in a climax as long in duration as it is powerful.

"I love you with all of my heart, Sophia," Kane says softly in my ear before he rolls to the side and takes me with him. He doesn't call me Tink, babe, baby, or Soph. Kane says my actual name so that I know that he means it and it make my heart feel so full that it aches. "Never doubt it."

I snuggle as deep into his side as I can get, and he tightens his arms around me when I whisper, "I love you even more, Husband."

Life with Kane as my husband will be anything but boring and maybe, just maybe, I am up for the challenge.

FIFTEEN

On hold and the magic of Magic the Gathering

Three days later . . .

"**A**nd this year's Winter Olympic Games are officially on hold pending the investigation into the murder of Germany's Layla Wagner," *the commentator on the news says.*

"Please turn that off," I say to Kane who is watching with rapt attention.

"Mrs. Wagner was found dead in her room at the village by the U.S. pairs skating team Dubois and Saucier, but we have yet to find out what they were doing in the Wagner's room that morning," *the other newscaster says.*

"That's true," *the man agrees before winking at the camera.* "Although there are rumors flying that half of the Dubois-Saucier team was having an illicit affair with Layla Wagner who was married to her partner, Johan, for thirteen happy years."

"Kill me now," I mumble to the ceiling because Kane is clearly not listening.

"Shh," he waves me off.

"I don't want to hear this," I tell him. The insensitive oaf has to know that this is hard for me to hear. "Turn it off."

"I know, baby," he says softly. "And I am sorry about that, but we need to know what they're saying about the key players in the case."

"Oh, okay," I capitulate.

"I'll make it up to you in a minute." He winks at me much the way the news anchor did before turning back to watch the show.

"That would be the hunky former hockey player turned pairs skater, Luc Saucier, am I right?" *the woman asks.*

*"*One in the same," *the man answers.* "Saucier once ruled the ice as a star in the professional hockey arena. But fights and scandal caused his team to withdraw his contract after one brutal fight ended the career of a fellow player."

"That player was Kane Green," *the woman says as they cut to an old PR photo of Kane from back when he was playing hockey.* "Green had the world of professional hockey at his fingertips but a particularly brutal fight with Saucier and another player left him with a shattered elbow."

"Green's hockey career ended that night," *the man says.* "But worry not, Sports Fans, he has been protecting the people of California for years now as a homicide detective."

They flash a recent paparazzi picture of Kane.

"Oh my," the woman says as she fake fans herself with her hand. *"He is dreamy."*

"Well, don't get too attached," *the man says.* "He married the other half of Dubois and Saucier this week. That's right, we have it on good authority that this ultimate bachelor was finally landed by the daughter of Senator Dubois of California."

"It's been a busy week for the duo from the United States." *the woman laughs.*

"I didn't land you," I practically shout at the screen. "He tricked me!"

Kane just laughs at my outburst.

"I bet those family Christmases are fun." *she winks.*

"Ugh. You don't know the half of it, lady," I groan.

"In an interesting turn," *the man says.* "It was a fight over Green's last wife that ended the friendship and Green's hockey career."

"Clearly, Saucier has a problem when it comes to married women," *the woman says.*

"I can only hope he gets the help that he needs soon," *the man says.*

"Are you kidding me!" I snap.

"This is bullshit!" Kane barks out.

"Join us tomorrow as we speak with the victim's husband, Johan Wagner, as he remembers his late wife fondly," *the woman says.*

"That's it for now," *the man says.* "Wishing you a good night for sports."

"That was a hatchet job if ever I saw one," Kane says as he points the remote at the TV to turn it off.

"It didn't look too great," I hesitate to agree. "But I'm hopeful that people will still give Luc a chance. Plus, who knows what we can find out."

"Yeah," he agrees with a grimace on his face.

"What should we do now?" I ask.

"There's not much more we can do about this until I hear back from my contacts," Kane says. "I could teach you Magic."

"As in the gathering?" I ask while shooting him a side eye.

"Is there any other kind?" Kane asks with his hand over his heart in faux shock.

"Fine," I sigh. "Do you worst."

"Oh, I plan on it." He smirks before grabbing a box of cards he had stashed in a duffle bag behind the sofa.

"This girl has ridiculous boobs," I inform him as I stare at the handful of cards he passed to me and then down to my own lacking endowments.

"She's a bad girl," Kane explains.

"And you like bad girls?" I ask.

"No, I like good girls who let me do very dirty things to them," he corrects me before placing a kiss on the tip of my nose.

"But you like huge boobs like this?" I ask as I flash him the card in question.

Kane sighs and rolls his eyes. "Soph, I'm going to tell you a secret about straight men," he begins, and I feel like whatever he says, I'm not going to like it. "We just like boobs. All boobs. Big boobs, small boobs, round boobs, squishy boobs, boobs bigger than my head, and teacup boobies that fit in my hand. Boobs are aweso—" I clap my hand over his mouth to stop him.

"I get it!" I shout exasperated. "You like boobs."

He licks my hand so that I pull it away from his mouth. "Honey, all straight men love boobs, but I love your boobs best."

"I have tiny boobs not huge . . . fun bags like this girl," I say with a little more insecurity showing in my words than I mean to and I tip my head to look away.

"Sophia, look at me," Kane says softly, and I lift my head to look into his baby blues. "You're perfect and I love you, every last bit of you. Okay?"

"Okay," I agree.

"This conversation is ridiculous," I inform him as I wipe my hand off on my jeans.

"Hey, you started it," Kane says with a twinkle in his eyes. "Are you ready to learn how to play Magic?"

"Yes! Fine. I'll learn. How hard can it be?" I snap.

"Okay, you have mountains and water and tree fungus . . ." Kane begins to explain.

"What?" I ask.

"Tree fungus," he says as he nods his head before whispering, "There's a fungus among us." And I can't help but laugh at his antics.

As it turns out, Magic is harder than it looks because Kane beat the pants off of me—*literally*—as I am not longer wearing pants. Who knew that nerds could be so dirty? I never should have agreed to stip Magic but I figured that nothing could be as complicated as Killer Bunnies. It turns out that I was wrong. Each game is as complex as the last.

"I don't know how I lost that last game," I say a little stunned as Kane dips his hand into the waistband of my panties.

"It's okay, I'll make it up to you," he says as he slides his fingers through the wetness between my legs. I let out a groan and squirm against his hand before he slips it back out of my undies.

Kane pulls the fabric down my legs and I whimper when the cool air hits my heated flesh before he rolls me to my hands and knees on the sofa. We never left the living room area of his suite and I find that now I'm not inclined to relocate at present.

"This might be fast, baby," Kane says from behind me. I hear the rasp of his zipper.

"Yes," I breathe as the blunt head of his cock touches me.

Kane grips my hips in his hands and slowly spears me with his hard length. We both groan as he slowly pushes all the way in and holds there for a moment. I squeeze around him and revel in the sound of his breath catching in his throat when I do. I love making the big, tough man—*my man*—lose his tight grip on his control.

He uses his hold on my ass to slide me almost all the way off of his length before slowly pulling me back. I arch into him and push back against him a little harder than he was leading me.

"That's right, baby," he rasps. "Fuck yourself on my cock."

So I do, I push back against my hold on the sofa cushions to slide myself off and onto his cock. The feel of him sliding across all of my favorite spots has me biting my lip to keep from calling out.

Kane bucks into me as I push back, and the feeling is off the charts. "I love it when you take what you want, baby. Take my cock."

"Yes!" I pant as Kane leans over me. The feel of his chest pressed against my back as he curls himself around me is indescribable.

He cups my breast with one hand and pinches my nipple hard between his fingers and I yelp and buck harder making him chuckle in my ear. But he does not speed up or pump harder. Kane does not give me what I want.

"Kane, please," I beg him. I would do anything in this moment to get Kane to let me come.

"Please, what?" he asks even though we both know that he knows exactly what I want from him.

"I need," I pant as he pumps faster and faster as he finally gives into what I want.

"I know what you need," he growls as he skims his

hand down my belly to between my legs.

"Yes," I cry as he presses down on my clit as he slides in and out between my legs.

My climax builds so fast and so strong that it steam rolls over me before I even realize it.

"That's it," Kane says into my ear as he drops his hand from between my thighs to brace against the sofa so that he has better balance.

His arms cage me in on either side of my body as he powers into me from behind. His thrusts so forceful that I have to drop down so that my breasts are pressed into the sofa cushions and I claw at the material with my nails.

Kane pumps faster and faster still bringing my passion for him back to life. I'm not sure that I could survive another climax of this magnitude but he won't let up. Kane gives me no quarter as he thrusts into me again and again.

"Kane—" I start. I don't even know what I'm saying, and I don't care. I just need him to end the burning inside me. I need to release it.

"One more," he groans as he drives into me again and again. "Give me one more."

"Kane! I can't," I call out even though we both know that it's a lie. My voice is muffled by the sofa cushions. "I'm close. I'm so close."

"I know you are," he says as he moves faster and faster hurtling us both toward the edge. "I need you to come."

Just then the door to the hotel room swings open and the entirety of the Dangerous Dames: Verna, Marla, Alyssa, Daisy, Shelby and even Trent file into the room and take a good look at us but I'm too far gone to do anything about it. I can't stop now.

"Oh, shit," Trent barks out a laugh. "Sorry, man."

"Get it, girl!" Daisy cheers.

"Everyone back outside!" Shelby says as everyone shuffles out the door.

"Now that's how you give me a great grandbaby," I hear Verna say as the door clicks closed.

"I-I'm c—" I start but I can't get any more words out because I do as I'm told and my jaw drops open and I moan as I come.

"Fuck, fuck, fuck!" Kane calls out as he plants himself deep inside me and follows me over the edge.

He drops the full of his weight over my back and I welcome it. I love this moment at the end when I can take all of him and hold him to me. It's a few seconds when our breathing matches and skin to skin, we are one. I hate that we don't have the time to bask in the closeness we share with each other, but our friends are waiting outside. The thought of them walking in on us has me face burning bright red with my mortification. If only the world would open up in a swirling vortex and swallow me whole right now, that would be great.

Kane eases up off of me and pulls out before standing up from the sofa to grab his jeans and pull them on sans underwear. I bury my face in the sofa cushions and groan. The world didn't open up into a swirling vortex and swallow me whole. One day I am going to stop wishing for things that I know won't happen.

"I'm going to need you to tell me that that didn't just happen," I say to Kane when I turn my head to the side, so I can breathe again and also watch as he pads across the room in nothing but bare feet and a pair of worn jeans to the bathroom. I hear water running and he returns with a damp washcloth that he gently uses to clean all evidence of him from my body.

I look into his laughing eyes and sigh. "I'm afraid that I can't do that, honey."

"I figured as much."

SIXTEEN

Bachelorettes and Big Thunder Oh my!

Twenty minutes later . . .

"**Y**ou guys can come back in now," Kane says as he holds the doorway open for the party of hooligans also known as our closest friends to enter.

"Hey, girl," Shelby says to me on a smile as walks in. Trent is right behind her wearing the most ridiculous smile I have ever seen in my life on his face. That can only mean bad things for Kane. Uh oh.

"What are you guys doing here?" I ask the room at large.

"Well, we were here to support you, obviously," Shelby answers.

"But now that the German ho got whacked and everything's on hold we decided to come hangout with our girl," Daisy finishes.

"Plus, you went and got yourself hitched to that

fine specimen of man meat over there," Verna says as she hitches a thumb towards Kane and I roll my lip into my mouth and bite it to keep from laughing. By the looks of him, Trent is not exercising that level of restraint.

"Seriously," Marla adds. "I hadn't ever gotten a good look at his ass before. But if I was thirty years younger—"

"More like forty years younger," Verna cackles. "And then you'd still be a cougar."

"Thanks, asshole," Marla replies to her best friend. "If I was forty years younger and still had two good hips, I'm not sure if I could live through that kind of pounding. But I'd love to try."

"Here, here!" Verna agrees.

"Nana!" Trent admonishes but his sweet grand-mother just shrugs her shoulders in a what-are-you-going-to-do-about-it kind of a way and joins in the laughter.

"Thanks, ladies," Kane says sweetly. "I think."

"Oh," Marla replies. "It was definitely a compli-ment."

My face burns bright red with mortification and I wonder if the Earth could please open up and swal-low me whole right now. That would be great. I realize when Verna replies that I didn't keep those thoughts in my head but instead shared them allowed.

"But if the Earth swallows you whole you can't get boned like that again," she adds not at all helpfully and everyone laughs.

"Granny!" Shelby yells.

"What?" Verna chimes back.

"You embarrassed Sophie!"

"Oh, pish posh," she says. "Sophie knows how much we love her and besides it's true."

"You guys love me?" I ask in a small voice and everyone turns to me with soft faces.

"Of course we love you," Shelby answers on a soft voice. "You're one of us."

"That's right, darling girl, you're a Dangerous Dame now and the only way out is toes first," Marla says.

"Jesus, Nana," Trent groans. "Stop threatening death."

"I'm not threatening anything," she says. "Being a Dame is dangerous work. I mean come on, it's in the name!"

And then I burst into tears. Loud body wracking sobs echo through the hotel suite.

"Shit," Kane barks just before he closes his arms around me like steel bands. "It's okay, honey. I won't let anyone kill you. I only just married you and I'd like to enjoy that for a good long while at least."

"We didn't mean to make you cry," Shelby says sounding a little panicked.

"I'm sorry!" Marla wails. "I forget what I'm saying sometimes. Of course, no one is going to kill you. Please don't cry!"

"Th-that's not why I'm crying," I sniffle.

"Well, then why, honey?"

"Because I've never belonged anywhere before," I answer and all the other women in the room burst into tears.

"Shit!" Trent barks out. "I don't know what to do with so many woman tears!"

"Well, buck up, fucker, and help me!" Kane yells at him.

"The Army didn't train me for this, you big hockey bastard!" Trent shouts.

"Would you stop calling me that!" Kane barks.

"I'm sorry that The Rangers, are manlier and therefore not as in touch with their feminine side as girly professional athletes," Trent says on a huff.

"Are you kidding me right now?" Kane growls.

"Noooooooo," Trent sing songs.

"I'm pretty sure you cried in your coffee at the station when Shelby didn't bring Miss home for the night," Kane tells the room.

"You shut your mouth right fucking now, Green!" Trent shouts.

"And aren't you the same guy who told anyone who would listen about home much your love that ugly ass cat?"

"She's not ugly!" Trent shouts. "Prepare for battle. Missy is the most beautiful cat in all of the world!"

"Son, that cat hit every branch of the ugly tree on her way down and that's what makes her cute," Marla says sweetly. "But she's still ugly."

"You betray me, Nana!" Trent wails as he clutches a hand to his chest in a mock display of being wounded.

"Shakespeare is rolling in his grave," I tell him on a laugh.

"When we get home, babe," Kane says to me and I see the mischievous twinkle in his baby blue eyes. "We should get a dog. Something manly like a German Shepherd."

"Or a cat just like Missy," I say on a wink.

"Hell, no!" Kane barks. "That cat claws anyone who's not Shelby. She doesn't even like Trent."

"And I call you all friends!"

"Trent! Kane!" Shelby shouts as she claps her hands stopping Trent from leaping across the room, bringing a halt to the fight that was already brewing.

"Damn," Alyssa mutters. "That was impressive. I like a gal who can take control of a situation."

"Thanks, girl," Shelby says on a smile before turning on the men. "Now, you two, hug it out."

"No," Trent says as he folds his arms across his chest.

"Him first," Kane grumbles.

"Pathetic, really," Verna says.

"True dat," Marla agrees and hold her fist up for a knuckle bump.

"I said," Shelby barks out. "Hug. It. Out. Now!"

Both Kane and Trent spring into action and give each other a quick man hug before jumping apart again.

"Now apologize!" Shelby issues her command worthy of any Drill Instructor. Both men kick and tow at the ground grumbling reasons why they shouldn't be the one to apologize and they sound just like a couple of five-year olds. Shelby narrows her eyes at them and the grandmothers cackle with glee. They know what's coming next. "I said now!"

"I'm sorry," Trent mumbles.

"Sorry, man," Kane grumbles so low that it's barely audible and my eyes water from trying to keep from laughing out loud at their ridiculousness.

"Now get out," she says on a saccharine sweet smile.

"What?" Kane asks.

"They have girl shit to talk about," Trent answers. "Let's go down to the bar and get a beer."

"Girl shit?" he asks.

"I don't know, man," Trent explains. "Girl shit. They probably want to know how big of a hockey stick you're swinging if you catch my drift. Although, we all know it can't be bigger than mine because I'm a God among men. And you know, they'll probably initiate her to the club and teach her how to maim someone with a supersized dildo or some other kind of giant rubber dick."

"Well, okay then," Kane says before coming to me and placing a small kiss on my lips. "Have fun."

"You too," I tell him.

"I will." Kane smiles at me. "And try and stay out

of trouble."

"How much trouble could a couple of octogenar-
ians get into?" I ask and loose some of the effect when
the ladies in question issue a series of guilty snickers
from behind me. "Forget that I asked that."

"Roger that," he says before following Trent out
the door. "And my dick is totally bigger!"

"They are ridiculous," Shelby says as she shuts the
door behind them.

"But they're your ridiculous," Alyssa says from
beside her.

"Now let's get down to business," Daisy shouts as
she pops the cork on a bottle of champagne. "You think
they got a sword in this here fancy ass hotel?"

"Uhh . . ." Shelby starts to answer. "Probably not.
Why?"

"I always wanted to try that dressage thing," she
says absent mindedly as she pours the champagne into
plastic glasses that Marla is unpacking from deep within the bowels of her gigantic purse.

"The horse dancing?" I ask.

"Horse dancing?" Daisy says incredulously. "Who
would want to dance with a horse? I don't even like
horses. What kind of crazy ass people dance with horses?"

"Dressage is a type of horse presentation," I explain and the women all look at me as if I have grown
a third head. "It literally means 'to turn out the horse.'"

"I don't want to turn out a horse or dance with it,"

Daisy says. "You're crazy. And I think I like it. I might kiss you later."

"Umm . . ." I stammer.

"It's best if you just go with it," Shelby whispers to me.

"Oh, okay," I say.

"You people are all crazy!" Daisy practically shouts. "Talking about dancing with horses. I just want to pop a champagne cork with a sword like a real pimp."

"Oh!" I say excitedly. "You mean sabrage!"

"That's what I said!" Daisy shouts. "Why are you guys never listening to me? I am full of knowledge and no one ever pays me no mind! You all are the worst. I don't even know why I put up with you all."

"Because you love us so much," Shelby says as she pulls Daisy into a tight hug. "What are you guys talking about?"

"Sabrage means to use a saber, or sword, to slice the cork off of a bottle of champagne in celebration. It would be cool to do but I doubt anyone would have a sword on them or let us borrow it even if they did."

"Oh," Shelby says as if I had just said the sky is blue today. "Sounds legit."

"None for me, thanks," I say as Verna tries to pass one to me. "I can't have a drink while training."

"But you're not training," Marla says. "Everything is on hold."

"That's true," I agree. "But until the competition is

over, I'm still in training."

"That sucks," Alyssa says.

"Eh, it's only a few more days."

"Now, where were we?" Shelby claps her hands again and I kind of feel like she missed her true calling as either a general in some kind of rebel army or a kindergarten teacher. When you stop and think about it, they're kind of the same thing anyways.

"Sophia was just about to tell us how big Kane's dick is," Verna chortles and my face burns scarlet again.

"Umm . . ." I start. "I don't know how to answer that."

"Well, you have seen it, right?" Verna asks, and Daisy laughs hysterically.

"Yes?" I answer.

"Girl, we just saw him drill you like an oilman!" Verna says on a laugh. "Now dish."

"Granny!" Shelby admonishes.

"What?" she shouts. "I could die tomorrow so I need the details today."

"You're not going anywhere, old woman," Marla laughs.

"He's . . . umm . . . he's good," I say softly to the chorus of whoops and hollers of all the women.

"I just knew that picture on the internet was true!" Daisy shouts.

"There's a picture of Kane on the internet?" I ask.

"Yep," Marla answers. "He's standing in a shower

in the altogether. Someone get me on the internet."

Marla waves a smart phone around while digging for something in her massive purse.

"Give me that," Verna demands as she snatches the phone out of Marla's hands. "And your glasses are on top you your head."

Marla immediately stops digging in her purse and pats the top of her head. When she finds a pair of reading glasses there, she pulls them down and puts them on her face before muttering what sounds like, "cranky bitch," under her breath.

I watch over her shoulder with the fixated attention that one might watch a car crash that is happening before them in real time on the highway as Verna unlocks the phone by sliding her fingertip across the screen and pulls up the web browser page. That happened one time. I was driving home from the rink when all of a sudden, a white Acura shot past me followed closely by three more vehicles. Illegal street racing is not uncommon in San Diego, but it is rare to see it at four o'clock in the afternoon.

I watched them fly down the highway weaving in and out of each other as the grappled for the prime spot in the lead when the Acura wobbled a bit and clipped a silver Honda Civic. Both cars flipped across the highway like skipping stones on a lake right in front of the afternoon traffic and I screamed before grabbing my phone out of the cupholder and calling the highway patrol. How both drivers managed to walk away is still a mystery to me and the universe. The way that I watched them fly down the highway is the same way I watch as one of my closest friend's grandmother looks up nude pictures of my husband on the internet.

She types "Kane Green Naked" into the search bar and then taps the link of "Images." A host of images of Kane in a small shower stall in various poses pops up. He has water cascading over his body. The muscles so honed they look as if they could cut glass. I let my eyes trail over every inch of the body that is still as magnificent now as it was then when he was a professional athlete.

Then I glance down to the object of everyone's fascination hanging between his legs. I thank God for small mercies that he is not erect in the photos because then I would have to be beating the throngs of sexually crazed women back with a stick—probably an old hockey stick because that would be poetic in this instance.

"Well?" they ask with rapt attention as they wait for my answer. "Is the picture real?"

I look back at all eight inches of him in his glory before looking back at all of my friends and nodding my head. "Yeah, it's real."

"Hot damn!" Verna shouts.

"Yeah, girl!" Daisy cheers. "My Jonesy is packing some serious heat too! How awesome is that?"

"Uhh . . . awesome?" I answer.

"Well, yeah," she says. "You don't know this on

account of you being a virgin an all when you hooked up with old, "Long Stick" here, but a little dick is not a good thing."

"Uhh . . ." I say not sure how to end this line of conversation. I shoot Shelby a "help me" look and she does anything but.

"Tell me about it," Shelby chimes in. "This one time, in college, I went to hook up with this guy who gave great sex-it-up text and when he got me to his apartment and I got naked, and then he got naked, I saw he had a pencil dick. It was awful!"

"Girl, what did you do?" Daisy asks.

"I took one look at it and put my clothes back on and went home. Ain't nobody has time for that mess," she cackles, and all the other women bust into loud, raucous laughter too. I, on the other hand, just sit there probably looking horrified because while I have no idea what they are all laughing about, I can surmise enough to know that I really don't want to know any-ways.

"No, you didn't!" Verna says.

"Of course, I did," Shelby laughs.

"That's my girl," Verna says on a sweet smile that she directs towards her granddaughter as if she had just won the Nobel Peace Prize.

"Let's get this party started!" Daisy shouts when everyone has a glass and I have a plastic bottle of water in my hands. "To Sophie and Kane!"

"To Sophie and Kane!" everyone shouts before

throwing back their glass of champagne.

Shelby runs around the room with another bottle and tops everyone off. When the glasses are all full again she raises hers in the air and shouts, "To Sophie!"

Everyone else raises their glasses and shouts, "To Sophie!" And I laugh.

Alyssa runs around filling all of the glasses one last time and when they're all full she raises hers in the air and shouts, "To the Dangerous Dames!"

"To the Dangerous Dames!" everyone shouts.

"And Big Thunder!" Daisy calls out. "Because everyone could use one. Except Sophie, because she's got Kane!" She breaks out into a fit of drunken giggles and we all laugh at her antics while my face burns beet red.

"And speaking of Big Thunder," Marla says on a hiccup. Apparently, these girls can't hold their champagne. "It's time we gave our girl here a lesson on all the things a happily married woman should know."

"Like what?" I ask. "Cooking?" They all die laughing.

"No!" Marla says. "Not cooking. I never cooked a meal the whole time my husband was alive that I didn't burn, and he never cared because we burned up the sheets if you know what I mean."

"Uhh . . ." I start.

"I'm pretty sure they burn up the sheets," Alyssa says. "At least by the looks of things."

"But variety is the spice of life," Verna adds. "And

that spice comes from dildos, nipple clamps, butt plugs, handcuffs . . ." she's listing them off on her fingers and I am growing more and more alarmed as she goes.

"Trent likes to use the handcuffs a lot," Shelby over shares. "But usually it's to lock me up somewhere. Although he hasn't really done that since James kidnapped me before he went on the lam. He's been really sensitive to that and I appreciate it."

"I've always wondered," Daisy asks. "Is it on the lam or on the lamb."

"I'm pretty sure it's on the lam and not like the adorably cute fuzzy baby sheep," Alyssa answers.

"Cool beans," Daisy says and I'm kind of glad she asked because I had no idea.

"I like a good nipple clamp," Alyssa adds to the mix.

"Oooh, those can be a little rough," Marla says. "But they can still be fun."

"That's alright," Alyssa says on a wicked smirk. "I like a little sting with my sweet."

"Well, I am here for the butt plug," Daisy crows and I want to crawl under the sofa and hide.

"Wh-what exactly do you do with that?" I ask hoping against hope that it's not for what I think it's for.

"It's to stretch your asshole out for when he wants to pound into your back door with that massive bacon torpedo of his," Daisy says on a sweet smile as she holds up the world's biggest chess piece.

"That looks like a giant bishop off of a chess

board," I mumble.

"Better this before his bald bishop rams the keep entrance," Verna says. "Plus, you start small and work up."

"Reading those sexy highlander books again, Granny?" Shelby asks on a giggle.

"Yeah," she answers. "How did you know?"

"No reason," Shelby laughs again.

"So . . . uhh . . . do you . . . uhh, do you use these?" I ask Shelby.

"Fuck no," she practically shouts as she answers me, and she gets so excited that she slides out of her seat on the sofa and lands in a ball of drunk girl. "There is no way that I would let Trent get his excreting eel anywhere near my pink starfish. Fuck that."

"What?" I ask sounding more than a little horrified because I am.

"His cock is like a baby's arm in a boxing glove," she explains in perfect intoxication that I'm not sure if I should be proud or terrified that I think I understand her.

"She's afraid her asshole will whistle when she poots," Verna rats out her granddaughter's biggest fear.

"You shut your damn mouth!" Shelby yells. "That is a legitimate fear."

I'm pretty sure that I agree with her. I don't know if I know what a poot is, but I'm pretty sure I don't want my asshole to whistle while I do it.

"I'm not sure I have what it takes for any of this,"

I say nervously.

"You don't have to either," Shelby smile sweetly at me. "You just have to love each other and have fun. That's all. Sex is whatever you make it."

I feel a frown pull on my face. I can't help but think about what Shelby said, but not in terms of Kane and me but Layla. From what I can tell, sex was more than just sex for her and I'm still not sure that I know what that means.

"What's got you down, sweet girl?" Marla asks me. "We didn't mean to upset you. You know that, don't you?"

"Of course," I answer here. "And you didn't upset me. I was just thinking about the murder."

"Now how in the hell can you be thinking about a murder when we're all talking about a little kinky good time fun?" Verna asks incredulously.

"Layla, the victim," I answer her. "Was tied up over a fancy wing back chair when she was killed."

"I still don't understand," Verna says.

"We're not making the leap with you," Shelby adds helpfully.

"Layla was naked and tied up for . . ." I drop my voice to a whisper. "Sex."

"Ohhhh," they all sing song in unison.

"So, it was a bondage thing?" Daisy asks.

"I don't know," I admit. "I don't know anything about that stuff. But she had ropes and knots all over. Including her breasts and her neck."

"Yep, that sounds like some kinky shit to me," Alyssa agrees.

"Can you explain it to me?" I ask softly. Suddenly I'm feeling really shy again.

"No," she answers me on a kind smile. "But I think he can." She points to the doorway where Kane and Trent are standing still laughing about something that must have happened in the bar downstairs. Well, not that I get a good look at them, Trent is laughing hysterically, and Kane looks less than impressed.

"What's going on?" I ask them.

"What's . . . what's going on . . ." Trent tries to get a handle on his hilarity as tears slips down his face and he struggles to catch his breath. "Is that there is a furry convention in this hotel."

"A what convention?" I ask. I have never heard of that word before. I mean some animals can be furry, right? But would someone have a convention of hairy animals? That seems odd.

"A furry convention is people who like to dress up in animal suits," Marla explains to me sweetly.

"Animal suits?" I ask for clarification because I am still not getting it.

"Like the kind mascots wear at high school football games," she explains.

"Or stuffed animals, or Care Bears, or Pokémon," Trent adds helpfully with a cheesy smile splitting his face, and Kane rolls his eyes.

"Like the kind with the big head helmets?" I ask.

"I mean I don't for sure, I went to a private boarding school for girls. We didn't have football games, but still."

"Exactly that," Marla says as she smiles brightly at me.

"But why?" I ask. I don't understand why anyone would do that.

"To fuck," Daisy says matter of factly as she examines her nails and I feel all the air in my lungs seize.

"What?"

"I know," she says. "It's weird. Now there is some real kinky fuckery out in the world and you didn't know about it on account of you livin' a really sheltered life and all so we're here to help you sort out the weirdness of life. Like people dressin' like stuffed animals to bang. That one I do not get."

"So why is this so hilarious?" I ask Trent who has to bend over and brace himself with his hands on his knees because he is laughing so hard he can barely stand.

"Because when we were downstairs, this woman dressed as a giant goldfish hit on Kane," Trent roars with laughter.

"And?" I ask. "I don't understand."

"It's only like, the worst Pokémon ever," Trent says as he rolls his eyes. "It has literally no effect and does no damage."

"Oh boy," Shelby says. "They're speaking nerd speak. We're in trouble now." And I can't help but laugh at that because not too long ago I was losing terribly as Kane tried to teach me another game. But truthfully, I don't mind. I enjoy those times with him and cherish them more than anything because he's showing me a part of himself. Kane is giving me pieces of him.

"So then," Trent carries on as if no one had interrupted him. "When Kane politely turns her down, she pats him on the chest and says, 'magic carp splash, but no effect.'"

"It was kind of awesome," Kane chuckles.

"It was classic," Trent agrees.

"They are so weird," Shelby says.

"Totally."

"But did you even splash, Bro?" Trent roars with laughter and Kane rolls his eyes before changing the subject.

"Now what was this about party favors?" Kane asks as he pulls me into his arms.

"Oooooohhh," the girls all call out.

"Looks like the party's over," Shelby says sweetly.

"Nah," Kane answers here. "It just became a private party."

"Sophie has some questions for you," Daisy says as she pats Kane on the chest before following the others out the door.

"Don't do anything I wouldn't do, kiddies," Trent laughs.

"That's easy," Kane says as he flips him off in a weird kind of good-natured way. "There isn't much you wouldn't do."

"That's true," he says on a smile before the door shuts in his face.

"Enjoy the party favors we left you," Alyssa shouts through the door and my face blisters.

"So, you have questions for me?" Kane asks with a smile in his voice and in his eyes as he steps towards me and wraps me up in his arms.

"Uhh . . ." I don't know if I can ask Kane my questions about the type of extracurricular activities that Layla enjoyed although I had earlier decided to ask him. I feel awkward and out of my comfort zone because I lack any type of knowledge in this arena.

"I missed you," he says as he breathes in the scent of my hair.

"I missed you too," I tell him as he starts walking me backwards in the direction of the bedroom.

"So, about these questions?" he asks, and I let out a nervous breath. "Don't be nervous, baby. Not ever with me. You can ask me anything." And in that moment, I know that I can.

"I didn't understand what you were asking Luc about how Layla like to have sex," I whisper and when a knowing look crosses his face I cringe a little. "I still don't."

"What don't you understand, honey?"

"I don't understand any of it," I tell him honestly as I push a frustrated hand through my hair. "I don't understand the rope or what it means. I don't know anything, and it makes me feel awkward and childish."

"You are neither of those things," Kane tells me. He lifts my chin up so that I look him in the eyes. "You are smart, sophisticated, and so fucking sexy that I'm always hard. It's like being a teenager again."

"Okay," I whisper.

"Do you want me to show you?" he asks softly.

"Show me?"

"Yeah," he says, his voice so soft I can barely hear him. "Do you want me to show you what it would be like to submit. Not like that, but the idea of submission?"

"I don't know," I answer honestly. "Can you explain it to me first?"

"Yeah, honey, I can," he says softly. Kane pauses for a minute before he continues his explanation. "If you were to submit for me, you would give your body and your trust over to me to know what you need to bring you pleasure."

"But what about you?" I ask, and he smiles.

"Don't worry about me. I would get mine by giving you yours, but also, I'd get off on controlling the situation."

"Huh," I say softly. "I did not see that coming."

"Do you want me to show you?" Kane asks.

"I-I don't know. I don't know if that's me."

"That's fine too," he says, and I can tell that he means it. "I'm okay with anything you want to do."

"I like what we do."

"I do too," Kane agrees on a sweet smile and I know that we'll be alright. "So, Alyssa says they left party favors? What's that?"

"Uhh . . ." I suddenly wish that I had drunk all the alcohol with the ladies. Darn my rule following ways!

"Where are they?" he asks me.

"O-o-on the coffee table." I have to clear my throat a couple of times because it keeps closing on me so I can't get the words out.

"I think I want to see what has my girl all tongue tied," he says as he lets me go and wanders back to the living room.

I wait for a few moments wondering what he's thinking as he's looking at all of the ridiculous shit that the Dames gave us as a wedding present. Thinking of the giant butt plug has my heart racing. I don't think I could ever want that back there.

"What the fuck?" Kane laughs loudly before calling out to me. "So, you said the girls gave you these things?"

"Uhh . . ."

"Babe," Kane says as he rounds the corner. "This has to be the biggest butt plug I have ever seen. This is ridiculous."

"The girls kind of scared me with that one a bit," I admit and cringe when he holds it up for further inspection in his hand.

"You don't need this," he says kindly.

"Good to hear it," I agree with him wholeheartedly.

"I'm glad to know that you're not interested in . . . uhh . . . the butt stuff."

"Oh, I'm interested," he says as he prowls forward, stalking me like a hungry lion would a wounded water buffalo. "But I will make sure you're ready for my cock when I fuck your ass. You don't need a bunch of plastic dicks because I'm better."

"Uhh . . . can I take your word for it?" I fidget feeling nervous and totally out of my element, not that anything sexy times is really my element. My only experience is what Kane has shown me so far and I'm totally okay with that.

"Or I could show you," he puts the idea out there. "I could warm you up so good with my mouth. I could eat you for hours while I slide my fingers one at a time between your sweet little ass cheeks and by the time that you come on my tongue you'll be begging for my cock."

"Uhh . . ." I'm practically catatonic as the images Kane spun swirl through my imagination.

"So, what do you think?" Kane asks.

"That sounds nice," I whisper.

"Yeah." And then his mouth is on mine as he kisses me hot and hard on hungry.

Kane pulls away from me in order to pull my t-shirt over my head. As soon as my face is uncovered again he rains kisses down all over my face. I push his t-shirt up over his abs and he reaches behind his neck in that sexy way that men do and pulls it the rest of the way over his head and drops it to the floor.

He reaches behind me and unsnaps my bra before I even realize that he's done it. The cool air of the room whispers across my heated skin and I suck in a quick breath before Kane puts his mouth to mine again. He unsnaps the button on my jeans and shoves them down my legs and I step out of them.

"Turn around," he says, and I move to face away from him without thinking about it. "Put your hands on the wall."

Kane covers my hands on the bedroom wall and slides them up to where he wants them on either side of my head, palms flat. After my initial hesitation, I can admit that Kane moving me around to where he wants me to be is kind of hot. Now if he tried it outside of the bedroom, we'd have problems.

He brushes my hair over my shoulder before he places open mouth kisses down the side of my neck and I lean into them. Kane places his warm palms over my belly as he sucks on the joint of my neck and shoulder.

He slides his hands up to cup my breasts and circles my nipples with his thumbs. Even though they are small, they feel heavy in his hands and I lean into his touch as he glides his nose against the skin behind my ear.

Kane slowly, oh so slowly, slides his hands down my body and into the waistband of my panties before pushing them down my legs when I step out of them and Kane kicks them away. He wedges is foot in between mine and nudges my ankles until I move my feet apart so that I am standing with my legs spread and my hands pressed against the wall.

And I am completely naked.

"Do you trust me?" he asks from behind me. He does not touch me, but I can feel the heat from his body as it burns into mine.

"Yes," I whisper. "I trust you."

Kane's only response to my words is to take my chin in his hand so that he can crush his mouth to mine over my shoulder. He licks into my mouth, swallowing my moans.

He moves his other hand to trail down my belly between my thighs as he swirls his fingers in the wetness he finds there. Kane doesn't start slow, but hard and fast as he circles my clit with his fingertip bringing me right to the knife's edge of my climax but instead of letting me topple over, he holds me there.

"Kane," I gasp but before I can reach the peak, he moves his hand away from my clit and slides his fingers deep inside my center. He pumps them in and out but he's careful to avoid the spot deep inside that makes me scream for him.

Just when I feel like I can catch my breath again, Kane pulls his fingers free and circles my clit again. I lean into the wall to help hold me up while he tortures me. Kane slides his other hand through the moisture between my legs before bringing it up to slide between my cheeks before dipping his smallest finger inside and I gasp. All of the air in my lungs whooshes out at once.

"Relax," he says as he trails kisses up the side of my neck and I do as he adds a second finger.

Slowly he works them in and out, stretching me as he goes. All the while his other hand circles my clit until I can hardly stand it. When I'm finally about to come Kane pulls away from me so that he's not touching me at all and I cry out in protest.

"Lay down on the bed," he tells me. His voice is rough with sex and need. "On you back."

I climb onto the bed and lay on my back just in time to watch him as he pushes his jeans down his legs. His cock is long and hard, but it's his eyes that watch me as he prowls towards the bed. Kane climbs up between my spread legs and leans forward to place a wet kiss between my thighs as he licks up my center until I can hardly breathe.

Kane sits up on his knees and reaches to the nightstand where he pulls out a condom and rolls it down his hard length. I watch as he produces a big tube of lube from the drawer and pops the cap. He turns it over and drizzles a large portion over himself and then even more between my legs. He lets it trail between my cheeks and then some.

I watch as he grips himself in his tight fist working the lube up and down his shaft. I roll my bottom lip between my teeth to keep from whimpering as I watch my husband. Then he turns to me with a knowing look in his eyes and pushes my knees up to my chest before he works the gel into my skin all around my clit driving me mad and then down to circle between my cheeks.

I feel the blunt head of his cock probe my entrance and I stiffen up. I'm so nervous.

"Relax, Tink," he says softly as he drops his thumb to my clit. "I won't hurt you."

It doesn't matter what he says because his thumb on my clit has everything else in my world out of focus. Kane slowly pushes into my entrance just an inch at a time and I gasp as it burns.

"Almost there," he pants as he pushes a little bit further and I feel full in weird places, but it's not bad.

He moves his fingers faster over my clit as he slips and slides in and out from my body. Kane slowly masters my body with a deep push and pull in the most intimate way. Just when I think to shy away from him and become skittish, Kane shows me that there is nothing I will hide from him.

"Fuck, Tink," Kane grounds out between clenched teeth as he pushes into me again and again. "I won't last." And it doesn't matter because neither will I.

I gasp, and I clench as I come with a hoarse cry and black spots cover my vision. Kane follows me over the edge with a roar.

After a moment our harsh breathing eases and Kane gently slides from my body before scooping me up into his arms like a bride. He carries me into the bathroom and sets me carefully onto the vanity while he reaches over and opens the taps to fill the massive tub with water.

When the water level is to his liking, Kane opens a bottle of bath oils and pours them in before lifting me back up into his arms and then stepping into the tub. He holds me in front of him as he dips a washcloth into the hot water and squirts some soap into it before gently scrubbing my body all over. He pays close attention to each of my breasts, the tips, now overly sensitive and I purr like a cat as he washes me all over.

When his hand drops down to wash between my legs, I am all but putty in his capable hands. He dips his fingers into my pussy and strokes me slowly and gently, in and out, in and out, until a soft climax washes over me. But it doesn't relax me, it energizes me. I am eager to turn the tables on my sexy husband.

I take the washcloth from his hands and turn to sit facing him in the tub on my knees. I pour more soap into the cloth and work it into a lather before scrubbing my husband's chest and rock-hard abs. Other things are now rock hard to a poking up above the water line, so I pour more soap directly into my hands and wrap both around him, one over the other and stroke him.

"Sophie," Kane groans as he rocks his hips in time to my hands. "Sophie, what you do to me . . . You feel so fucking good."

"I aim to please," I whisper as I watch my hands move over his hard flesh.

"And please me, you do, baby," he says as he stiffens even further. "So fucking much."

"I'm glad," I say as I work him harder and faster.

"Baby," he rasps, his voice heavy with sex. "I'm going to come in your hands if you don't stop right now."

"That's the idea," I whisper. "I'll catch you when you fall."

Kane crushes his mouth to mine as he growls his completion between us and we stay like that for a while, just holding each other. I love the quiet moments after where it's just us skin to skin.

The water has grown cooler and we wash quicker before Kane pulls the plug on the drain and scoops me up to carry me out of the tub just as he carried me in. The tender gesture does more to warm my heart.

He quickly towels us off before carrying me back to bed where he holds me in his arms all night and it's exactly where I want to be.

SEVENTEEN

Practice, practice, practice, and spit in your
eye

This morning I woke up ready to take on the day and the day in question promptly spit in my eye.

Verna always tells me that in life you have to wish in one hand and shit in the other and that life will show you which one will fill up faster. As crude as that analogy is, it's not wrong. I had pretty big hopes and wishes that I laid down on today and I was wrong.

I was so totally wrong.

After spending yesterday with friends celebrating my marriage—no matter how big of a surprise it may have been to all of us—and a night spent in Kane's arms I felt ready to take on the world. Even though the Games were on hold and Luc was in a tenuous situation, I was okay, I felt content. I felt like maybe everything would be alright.

Then late last night, Olympic officials called around to notify all of the competitors that the Games would resume first thing in the morning. I was ecstatic. I have been ready for this final skate for ages because in truth I have been preparing for it my whole life.

So instead of sleeping in my new husband's arms, I packed my things and headed back to my room at the Olympic Village. My roommate was more confused than happy to see me which seems weird. Something is off with her and I don't know what.

"What are you doing here? I thought the news said that you married the hockey god?" she had asked me when I walked through the door.

"Apparently, I did."

"What?" Natalie had asked me.

"It's a long story," I had vaguely explained.

"Cool," she had said with a strange look on her face.

And then I had put my pajamas on and set my alarm for early in the morning because Luc and I had a very early call for a practice in the morning. I probably should have spent more time with her, delved deeper into what was going on with Nataliewhile I was off with my friends during the hold they had placed on the Games.

But I didn't and now I would probably never know.

Beep . . . beep . . . beeeeepp . . .

My alarm sounds in the dark of the early morning at my room in the Village. I reach over a quickly silence it so not to wake up my roommate. She has a practice later today and needs her rest. We were up later than I had wanted last night so that she could ask me all kinds of questions about life with Kane. She has been so nice to me and so sweet that I wouldn't deny her anything for fear of hurting her feelings. I am hopeful that we can be friends when we return to the United States.

I quickly hop out of bed and head into the bathroom to brush my teeth and wash my face before securing my hair in a ballet bun on top of my head. I move through my makeup routine with a practiced hand as I apply more rouge than one of the crazy old ladies that lives in the same retirement condos as Verna and Marla. I pop open my favorite eyeshadow palette and swish my brush in the compressed powder before swiping it over my eyelids. I top it all off with a little mascara and lipstick before stripping out of my pajamas and pulling on a pair of tights and another practice dress. I slide my feet into my chucks and pull on a coat before tossing my skate bag over my shoulder and heading out the door.

Today is going to be a great day!

I walk to the bus stop where I hop on the bus. It was

waiting there, and I have this feeling that everything is going to be alright.

"Thank you," I say to the bus driver on a bright smile before hopping off the bus at the practice arena.

When I walk inside, Kane, Luc and Eugen are all there waiting for the practice to begin. Kane and Eugen sip from paper coffee cups while Luc holds a plastic water bottle in his hand. All of our competitors, save Johan and Layla for obvious reasons. And those reasons are she's dead and he's grieving although from what I saw while the Games were on a hold, I'm not so sure that I believe that last part.

We all head into one of the locker rooms where we have been assigned spots to get ready however we need to. We drop our skate bags to the rubber mats covering the floor before moving to a small space in the corner to block out our long program in our sneakers. We only have today and one more day before it's all over, so we need to make the most of our time.

I can't quite put my finger on what it is, but something seems off with Luc and it worries me. But I don't have time to borrow other troubles, so I push it out of my mind and move on.

Twenty minutes later and I would wish I hadn't.

We move back to the bench and sit down. I kick my chucks off and lace up my skates. I pop in my earbuds so that I can't hear the other skaters milling around and walk through my stretches to warm up my body before it's time to take the ice.

Before too long Kane places his hand on my arm and I pull the earbuds from my ears and pause my music.

"It's time, honey," he says softly.

"Thanks," I say as I smile at him.

I wrap my earbud cords around my phone and hand it to Kane. As I do I have the funniest thought float through my head that when we get home, Kane and I have to figure out how to combine our lives for good in a way that we can both live with for hopefully, as long as we both live. Most of it is silly stuff like cell phone plans and homes.

I hand my phone to Kane and he tucks it into his jacket pocket. I pull off my fleece jacket and stuff it into my skate bag before following Luc out of the locker room and down the hall to the rink gate. The French team, the Russian team, and the Korean team are all already standing by the gate waiting for it to open. When Luc and I walk up, all conversation comes to a halt.

Thankfully, we don't have too much time to dwell on it because the Committee Official has come to open the gate to the ice. Our last official practice has officially begun.

We all take the ice and Luc and I take several laps to warm up before moving into a series of more complicated maneuvers. Luc takes my hand in his as we move diagonally down the rink and we move through one of the footwork sequences of our long program. Instantly, I notice that our timing is not in sync. It also becomes obvious when the blade of Luc's skate clinks against mine and he knocks my feet out from underneath me and I tumble to the ice.

"Shit," Luc barks as he scoops me up off the ice.

"It's okay," I say softly as I brush off my bruised backside. "Let's just move on."

"Alright," Luc replies gently before taking my hand and leading me into our side by side jump combinations.

The first jump we move through beautifully but the second, he's too close to me, something I notice the second my feet leave the ice. His jump trajectory is towards me instead of moving alongside me in the same direction. We're going to collide and there is nothing I can do to stop it, I can only brace.

When we hit the ice in a heap it feels like all of the bones in my body smash together and then pop out again. The feeling is quite jarring. It takes me longer to get up from the ice this time and I feel the eyes of all the other people in the rink and on the ice watching this disaster. My little tiny tots that I teach to skate are usually much better than Luc and I are skating right now.

Luc pushes up from the ice and brushes off his pants before offering me a hand to help me up and I do the same.

"Should we—" Luc starts to ask. I know that he wants to ask if we should end this practice early and I just can't bear to give in to defeat so I stop him before he can finish his request.

"No," I deny. "Let's just keep going."

"Alright," he says again before taking my hand and leading me around the rink to lead me into a throw axel.

Luc grabs me by the waist to step forward and throw me up into the air and as soon as his hands let go of me, I can tell that he's thrown me too high and too far. I hit the ice on my right hip and pain blasts through my leg. It's not broken, but the break to my leg that has healed sings in pain.

I hear Kane let out a roar as I push myself up. I don't want Luc to feel bad, but also, I'm done here today. My only hope is that I'm not done here—period.

"I'm okay," I tell Luc. "But I think we're done here today."

"I'm so sorry," he tells me as we make our way off of the ice.

"It's okay.," I say to Luc before mumbling to myself. "I need to ice my ass . . . or my whole body." It feels like the whole of me will be black and blue by sun down. I'm moving like I'm one hundred years old. Marla moves faster than I do right now, and she has a bad hip. I can see by the look on his face that Luc feels bad and it's not his fault. There is a lot going on here and we're both distracted. I can only hope that after a good night's sleep we are ready to rise to the challenge and compete tomorrow.

"It's not fucking okay," Kane clips out and I know that he's worried but I need him to calm down.

"Shhh," I try to quiet him. "You're making a scene."

"I don't fucking care," Kane growls. "You could have killed her."

"I think that's being a little over dramatic," I say as I roll my eyes.

"Well, I don't," he bites out.

"I know and I'm so sorry," Luc says. I turn to tell him to stop apologizing but when I look at him something is wrong. His coloring is all off and he looks like he's barely standing.

"Kane," I say trying to get his attention.

"I see it, honey," he tells me and thank God because something is not okay right now.

"I don't feel so—" Luc starts to say before he collapses at my feet.

"We need a medic!" Kane shouts before dropping to his knees to give Luc the emergency aid that he needs until the medics get here.

Kane puts his ear to Luc's chest with a scowl on his face before nodding to me. At least he's still breathing. Poor Luc. He places his fingertips to the side of Luc's throat and turns the wrist of his free hand to see the face of his watch as he watches the second-hand tick around.

Kane lifts Luc's eyelid and the man of the hour blinks a few times. His gaze is still foggy, and his pupils are big.

"What did you take?" Kane demands and Luc licks at his dry lips.

"What?" he mumbles.

"I asked you what did you take?" Kane says through gritted teeth. He's barely holding onto his anger. I don't understand how he could think that Luc would take drugs before stepping on the ice.

"Nothing," he rasps as if his tongue is too big for his mouth and he struggles to speak around it.

"If I find out you took something before getting on the ice with Sophia, I will kill you," he grounds out.

"Kane!" I whisper shout to get his attention. "Luc wouldn't do that, and you know it."

"I don't know anything," he says to me as he steps back to let the medics in to take Luc to the hospital. "But I will stop at nothing to keep you safe."

"I'm safe, Kane," I tell him gently.

"You're mine, Tink. And you're going to stay that way."

"Okay, Chief," I whisper as I touch his cheek softly. "So, you really think Luc was drugged?"

Kane lets out a sigh and runs his hand through his hair before answering me. "If he didn't take something himself, then someone slipped him something."

"But what could he have had?" I ask.

"My guess is it was slipped to him right before he got here or right as he got here," Kane answers my question.

"But what could that have been?" I ask

It's like in the old Saturday morning cartoons where the light bulb suddenly flashes of the character's head when they figure something major out. Both Kane and I jump up at the same time and shout, "The water!" before we take off for the locker room.

Kane pulls at a roll of paper towels hanging on the wall in the corner before lifting the lid off the trash can. Fortunately, it's so early in the morning that there isn't a lot of garbage in the trashcan yet. Just the coffee cups, a water bottle, and a takeout bag. He uses the paper towels to lift the water bottle out of the trash can and holds it up to the light to inspect it.

"Well, I'll be damned," Kane mumbles more to himself than to me.

"What?" I ask as I step closer to get a better look.

"Do you see the little particles stuck to the inside of the bottle?" he asks me.

"Yes."

"That's not something you should see in a toss away plastic water bottle," he explains. "Someone put something in his water."

"Oh no."

"Yeah," he says softly. "Grab me one of those plastic laundry bags, would you?"

I look over to the wall where Kane is pointing to and see the locker rooms have plastic laundry bags hanging on the wall. I grab one and hold it open, careful not to touch the inside of the bag. Kane gently places it in the bag before pulling his phone from his pocket and calling his contact at the police department here. Leave it to Kane to make contacts wherever he goes.

By the time the police had arrived, Luc had been transported to the hospital where he was declared to be fine and sleeping off the effects of an Ambien. To my knowledge Luc wasn't a big user of sleep aids but he was under extreme pressure while being accused of murder. Who am I to say how someone else would react in that situation? There was also the matter of the substance in the water bottle which the police happily took as potential evidence.

"Who would do such a thing?" I asked Kane as we left in a private car to head back to his hotel.

"Whomever stands to gain from Luc looking like a reckless killer," he answered, and I gasp.

"You think it's the killer?" I asked.

"Yeah, honey."

"But who is that?" I ask still feeling the surrealness of the situation.

"I have my ideas on the matter," Kane says vaguely.

"Who would want to kill Layla?" I ask.

"Her husband," Kane answers me.

"But without her, he can't compete," I say trying to wrap my mind around the facts at hand. "That doesn't even make sense.

"You guys were poised to win," Kane says. "They were never going to catch up in the ranks if you skated like you did in the short program. His chances were over."

"They still could have won the silver," I answer. "And no one knows how a skate will go. We can't guarantee a win. Just look how we skated at practice this morning."

"Yeah, but you had help in that area," he drolls.

"True." After a moment I say, "But Johan wasn't at the rink. How could he have drugged Luc?"

"That's what we have to figure out," he says before leading me through the paparazzi at the entrance to his hotel.

Kane ushered me onto the elevator where we rode up to his floor. I find a certain level of comfort just being near him and the way that he wraps his arm protectively around me helps too. He slides the key card from his pocket and unlocks the door. Kane holds it open and motions for me to move inside first. He lets the door shut behind him and flips the lock over.

"I feel numb." I tell him. "I don't know what to feel."

"Worried over the wellbeing of your friend?" he asks. "Helpless. Overwhelmed."

"Yes, to all of those things."

"He should be okay," Kane tells me as he wraps me up in his arms. I tuck my head against his broad chest and just let myself feel as if I could absorb some of his strength through osmosis or something. I'm not really sure because I barely passed chemistry in high school so who knows really?

"Let's get you into bed, baby," Kane says to me softly.

He pulls my jacket off of me and tosses it over a

chair in the room before taking my hand in his and leading me into the bedroom. I kick off my chucks as Kane pulls the pins from my hair and lets it fall down around my shoulders in a heavy mass. He gently tucks his finger into the neck like of my practice dress and pushes it off of my shoulders and down around my ankles. He takes my tights with him and I hear him suck in his breath when he sees that without my skating dress and tights I am completely naked. Even though his eyes heat when he takes in my nudity, Kane gently pulls his long-sleeved t-shirt over his head and rolls it up to drop it down over my head. He's so much bigger compared to me that the hem falls around my knees.

He reaches over to the bed and pulls down the covers letting me climb in before pulling them back up to tuck me in. He pads softly into the bathroom and I let my body sink down into the mattress and goose down comforter and pillows as I hear water running. When he comes back a moment later, he's carrying a damp washcloth. Before I have a chance to ask what he's doing, Kane sits beside me on the edge of the bed and delicately wipes away my makeup.

"Thank you," I say softly, and he just nods before heading back into the bathroom to deposit the washcloth.

"Let me know when you're hungry and I'll order room service for dinner," he softly commands. "Until then just sleep. You're safe with me."

Those words echo in my head, pinging around like

a pinball. *You're safe with me.* And I know that I am. Kane won't let anything happen to me. I am totally taken care of, so I do what he says and close my eyes to sleep.

Kane has it covered here. Tomorrow will be better.

I can only hope.

Too bad I would only find out how very wrong I was . . .

EIGHTEEN

Perfect Score

Today is the day.

All the training and the practices, every early morning skate, all of the tears and sweat and bloodied feet were all to get to this moment. Today is the long program skate for this year's Winter Olympic Games.

Luc and I stand with Eugen as we prepare to take the ice one last time. The French team sits in the kiss and cry and well, it's definitely a cry. She is sobbing loudly and uncontrollably as their coach looks on with a horrified expression frozen on his face. The reason why is there for all to see. Their marks were harsh. There's no other way to describe them. I'm not actually sure you could even step on the ice and receive a score so low for just showing up.

It had to be a bad omen, I'm sure.

This last week has been an exercise in both patience and frustration as we both waited to hear the fate of Luc but also if the competition would resume before the true killer was caught. If the killer is ever caught. Either way, the authorities let Luc go to resume competition and for that I am grateful.

Two nights ago, long after the impromptu party with the Dames had ended and Kane had finished loving me into the night, we were notified that the Games would resume in the morning. Luc and I were scheduled for a six o'clock practice time and the final skate at four this afternoon. So off I went back to my room in the Olympic Village to get a decent night's sleep away from sexy retired hockey player husbands who had ideas for late night activities other than sleeping.

The next morning, everything should have gone as planned. Luc and I could skate our long program forwards and backwards, but something was off. He was out of time and we were out of sync. It was when he dropped me—repeatedly—that I knew we were toast. But when he collapsed after we left the ice, Kane and I realized quickly that there was foul play a foot. The questions remain who and why? I still don't have the answers to those questions and now here we are, preparing to step on the ice for the last time.

I can only hope that today will go better than yesterday did.

"Yesterday is gone," Eugen says in his accented English. "Today is all you have."

Luc and I both nod because he's not wrong.

This morning I woke up in Kane's bed at the hotel, usually a no-no at elite competitions such as the Olympics, but when there is a murderer on the loose and your partner is drugged, you get to stay cuddled up against you police detective husband.

Desperate times calling for desperate actions and all that jazz . . .

As it turns out, I was so exhausted from all that had been going in at these Games and all of the drama in my life that when Kane tucked me into his bed and told me to sleep I did. And when he told me to get up when I was hungry, well, I didn't do that because I slept through the night and on into the morning.

When I finally woke up it was time for a healthy breakfast and to begin my preparations for the long program skate. So that's exactly what I did.

I got up and showered while Kane ordered a light breakfast, something to power me through the day but not weigh me down. This is one of the times that dating a former athlete really come in handy. Although, I guess we're not dating anymore, come to think of it.

I took special care to wrap my body in one of the big fluffy bath towels while I dried my hair and then pinned it up in a big ballet bun on top of my head. I usually would not have washed my hair to then junk it up with gel and hairspray, but I needed the shower to wash the last of the sleep away from my body.

Kane and I had sat in the small table off the living room and dined quickly and quietly. Today is not a day for distractions. I need to shut out all thoughts of the case and keep myself in the right headspace.

After we finished eating breakfast, Kane cleared the room service cart back into the hall and called them to come pick it up while I went back to the bathroom to brush my teeth and start my makeup. Competition day makeup is so thick and dark that it would make a drag queen jealous. I started with a setting spray that is basically super glue and then set my foundation and base on top of it. I used enough bronzer on my forehead and under my cheekbones to look like I've just come from Barbados even in winter and a peach blush on the apples of my cheeks. I opened my eyeshadow palette and slicked my eyelids with a shimmery pink eyeshadow all over the lid and a deep plum over the outside corners and crease to smoke it up a bit. I topped it all off with black eyeliner and mascara. My eyelashes are so thick and long that I have never had to wear fake lashes and I consider myself lucky.

I pull a new pair of tights up my legs and slip my program dress off of the hanger in the closet before stepping into it and pulling it up my body. It's a bright royal blue with a long chiffon skirt that fades in an ombre to a baby blue so light in color that it's almost white. The body of the dress dips in a deep vee in the front and the back but has an invisible nude body that holds it on. White crystals and beads in varying sizes are all along the trim of the dress. I slid my arms into the short sleeves before I padded over the Kane in my stocking feet.

"Will you zip me up?" I had asked. "Please."

"Anything for you, Tink," Kane had said on a smirk just before I turned around and presented him my back to zip up my dress.

"Thank you," I had said on a small smile before pulling on the matching blue bands that circle my upper arms and then my Team USA warm-ups over my dress. I stepped into my favorite chucks before I called out to Kane. "You ready to go?"

"Babe," he had said, and I could see the laughter in his eyes as he stood there in worn jeans that cupped him in magnificent places, a burgundy long-sleeved t-shirt, running shoes, and a fleece pull over. He had his Team USA coat over his arm and a paper travel coffee cup in his hand.

"I guess you're ready to go then," I had said and then we walked out the door to head to the rink for the final skate of the final competition of my skating career.

"And now, representing the United States of America," *the announcer says.* "Sophia Dubois and Luc Saucier!"

"Let's do this," Luc says to me and I smile brightly at him.

"Let's."

The official opens the gate and we step onto the ice. Luc takes my hand in his and leads me around the rink in a quick warm-up lap before stopping us at our opening spots. He swings me out and then spins me back in to signal the start of our music.

While the Bonnie and Clyde theme of our short program was upbeat and fun, we decided to show the full range of emotions with our long program and I had had this idea to present a couple who did not work out but love each other with all of their hearts as we skate to *Break Up in the End* by Cole Swindell.

I remember years ago, I was a bridesmaid in a friend's wedding and one of the couples that was friends of the bride and groom were in the process of separating and eventually divorcing. It was so beautifully painful to watch them walk down the aisle together knowing that afterwards, they were going their separate ways. I happened upon them on my way to the bar as they held each other and cried together. You could feel how much they still cared for each other but even through all of that, love just wasn't enough and it was as devastating as it was poetic. I channeled those emotions while choreographing this program.

Luc and I stand back to back and as the opening strains of the song begin, we circle around each other. He hooks his skate to mine and we swing around before unhooking out feet and joining hands to skate down the diagonal of the rink and move into our side by side jump combinations. Luc and I land at exactly the same time. Neither of us falter or stumble. The jumps are the cleanest we have ever done, and I close my eyes for a second to say a silent thank you.

He picks me up into a hand to hand lasso lift before he tips me forward into a star lift as he skates down the ice. Luc flips me forward over his shoulder and holds me to his side where I draw my legs up into a cuddle position before he sets my feet back on the ice.

Luc takes my hand in his as we skate backwards together. I lift my leg into an arabesque before he flips me around into a death spiral and as I always do when we execute one of these moves, my stomach drops to my toes for a split second before we pull out of the element.

We skate the rest of our program without a single hitch and when Luc tosses me into an axel I can't help but let a huge smile split my face when I land. He expertly leads us through a romantic footwork pattern as the music winds down to a close where we almost slow dance around the rink before finally turning away from each other and I wrap my arms around my middle as the music ends and the couple we play finally gives up on each other.

When the roar goes up from the crowd Luc pulls me into a huge hug and holds me tight before taking me by the hand and swinging me around so that we can bow to the judges and then spinning me around to bow to the audience.

All the while the crowd chants *"USA! USA! USA!"* I have to bite my lip to keep from crying and I know that before the day is out I will be bawling like a baby. There is this weird emotional roller coaster that you ride when you have all of the adrenaline and endorphins coursing through your body only to finally crash. To top it all off, this is my final Games. I am saying goodbye to this part of my life, I'm closing the book on my competitive career and starting a new chapter as a married coach.

As Luc leads me off the ice I look over and see Kane sitting in the front row with Trent and all of the Dangerous Dames. His broad smile splits his face from ear to ear and a tear runs down his cheek as he mouths "I love you," to me.

I smile and mouth the words back just before we step off of the ice and head to the kiss and cry to find out our fate. Our skate was damn near perfect and the crowd went wild but all that could mean nothing if the judges were left unimpressed.

I sit between Eugen and Luc on the bench as we await out scores. One of the girls from the local skating club walks up to hand me flowers and a teddy bear that she has collected from the ice and I reach out to take them from her with a smile on my face. I offer her one of the bears from the stash and she smiles huge and nods before taking her treasure and walking away.

My heart is pounding in my chest and my palms are sweaty. I don't know of a time in my life when I have been more nervous or scared but I sit there with a serene smile on my face even if it's fake. The world will think that I have everything under control when in reality I am a basket case on the inside.

"And now," *the announcer says, and I close my eyes.* "For technical . . . 10.0 . . . 10.0 . . . 10.0 . . ."

I gasp and have to cover my mouth with my hands as the marks go on and on.

"And for artistic . . . 10.0 . . . 10.0 . . . 10.0 . . . 10.0." *This is insane. Our program was amazing, and all our hard work is finally paying off.* "The Americans take the Gold."

Luc and I were the last skate of the day so those are the final standings for the Pairs Skating competition and Luc and I just won.

They escort us to the winners' podium where the French team and the Canadian team are already standing there. The French had placed second and the Canadians third.

"Congratulations," they each say to us as Luc and I take our places at the top.

"Thank you," I say to each of them. "Congratulations also."

I'm practically shaking when the Olympic official places the medal around my neck and hands me a bouquet of roses. I'm a quivering mess. I hold them in my left arm and place my right hand over my heart as the American Flag is lowered from the ceiling and it hangs higher than all of the others.

Hot tears roll down my cheeks as the Star-Spangled Banner is played. My heart is so full of pride for my country and the knowledge that Luc and I have represented the United States well.

This is it. We did it. Luc and I went out in a blaze of glory.

And just like that we took home the Gold.

And now it's time to celebrate.

CHAPTER 19

Something weird when you bless the rains and undeserved celebrations

"Let's get this party started!" Shelby shouts when we walk in the door.

After the medals ceremony we changed into street clothes and left the arena to meet our friends at the tavern. I wore my medal over a black and gray striped cowl neck sweater, dark skinny jeans, and black ballet flats under a light pink wool coat.

We were stopped by fans to sign autographs and the whole thing was surreal. I haven't stopped smiling since the medal ceremony.

Luc, Kane, and I all piled in a cab and headed around the corner to the tavern. When we walked in the door a cheer went up through the crowd in the bar. It makes me want to cry all over again.

"Babe," Kane says on a laugh. "You only just now stopped crying."

JENNIFER REBECCA

"I can't help it," I tell him and Luc laughs. "It's happy tears."

We walk over to the tables where our party is seated, and Kane takes his coat and mine and hangs them on the backs of our chairs. We are greeted with hugs and cheek kisses from everyone before we sit down at the table. I would wish much later that I had paid more attention to who was in the bar and who was paying attention to our party instead of being in the moment and basking in celebrating with our friends.

"Barkeep!" Marla calls out and I laugh when I realize while Luc and I were wrapping up the last of our official obligations for the day, the Dames had already gotten their party started. "We need shots!"

"Ungh," Trent groans and shoots Kane a disgruntled look.

"What?" Kane laughs. "Dude, she's your grandmother."

"And I love you like you were my own grandson," Marla smiles at Kane and hugs her.

"You guys are all drunk as skunks," I tell them on a laugh.

"Yep!" Shelby agrees with a snicker. "Time for you to catch up."

"Thank you," I smile to the waitress as she passes us all glasses of champagne and tequila shots. I'm not sure if the two go to together but I have also never won the Olympics before, so this is a learning experience for all of us.

"To Sophie and Luc!" Verna calls out as she shoots back her tequila.

"To Sophie and Luc!" everyone else calls out as they throw back their shots. Luc and I laugh as we throw back ours too.

I look to Kane who has his arm behind me, loosely on the back of my chair. His eyes are warm as he smiles at me. I could get lost in those eyes and thankfully, I get to for the rest of my days.

"I'm so glad you're here with me," I tell him honestly and it's true.

"Tink," he whispers as he cups my cheek and places a loving kiss on my lips.

I'm so glad to get to share this moment with him. A lot of men would have a hard time being in the background and Kane has been the perfect supportive partner. It was an interesting flip to my dad's side of telling me not to embarrass him and to represent him well.

"I need some food before I fall over," Shelby says before she lets out a massive belch worthy of a truck driver. I feel my eyes go wide because I've never actually heard someone burp like that before. "Excuse me."

"That's impressive," I tell her.

"Thanks?" she laughs.

"Think you can teach me how to do that?" I ask. "Never mind. That might be the tequila talking." I look over at Kane and his shoulders are bouncing as he silently laughs at me.

"What?" I ask him.

"Nothing," he says on a smile. "You're cute when you're drunk."

"I'm not drunk," I explain. "I'm tipsy."

"Okay, you're cute when you're tipsy," he corrects. "Just don't get too drunk. I'm looking forward to fucking Tipsy Sophie later."

"Okay," I breathe feeling the air sear my lungs.

"What can I get everyone?" the waitress asks when she comes back to the table.

"A steak and a baked potato, please," I say as I hand her my menu. Even though we're in another country, I order a steak because I deserve a darn good meal after all we've been through. Also, because a steak and a baked potato are pretty hard to mess up. The tequila is also hitting me pretty hard, so I feel like I need something pretty substantial to line my stomach so that I don't make a fool of myself and can make it to the drunk sex portion of the evening with Kane.

"I'll have the same," Kane says from beside me as he hands his menu to the waitress.

"Me too," Luc says also.

"I'll have a burger, please," Trent says.

"I'll have the grilled chicken," Alyssa orders.

"Ohh, me too," Shelby says. "That looks so good."

"I'd like a burger, too, please," Verna says. "With mayo. Do you have mayo?"

"Yes," the waitress answers. "We have mayo."

"I'd like some on my burger, please."

"I'd like the same," Marla says.

"Better make it three," Daisy adds completing our dinner order.

"I'll have that right out," the waitress says before she leaves.

"Ooohhh," Kane says excitedly. "They have karaoke!"

Kane jumps up and hustles on over to the DJ with the song book and I laugh. He's like a little kid on Christmas morning. I hear the opening to his song and I know, I just know. I will never not associate this song with Kane and sex in the back seat of his car.

"Your boy is about the bless the rains again," Daisy tells me.

"I know," I say on a laugh.

"And I am here for that!"

"I'm glad," I tell her.

"Just wait until you see her man sing Africa," she tells Alyssa.

"Really?" she asks with a laugh.

"Oh yeah," I tell her. "It's ridiculous."

"Awesome," she says as she sits back in her seat to enjoy the show.

"I need more champagne for this show of male prowess," I tell Alyssa. "I'll be right back."

I grab my champagne glass and head for the bar but when I get there, I wish that I had stayed in my seat. Johan is obviously drunk—and not the happy fun times drunk like my friends, but the angry I'm going to take everyone down and make a scene drunk—at the bar.

"I see you're still hanging around the man who murdered my wife," he sneers.

"Luc didn't do it and you know it!" I practically shout. How dare he stand here and cause another scene. Why doesn't he just go back to his home?

"I don't know it," he challenges me and there is a weird glint in his eyes. Something is off, and I can't quite put my finger on it.

"You know what I think?" I push him. "I think he liked her. And I know Luc wouldn't hurt a fly."

"You sure about that?" Johan asks and by the look on his face, I can tell that he is about to drop a verbal bomb on me. Something that will shake up everything that I know. I just don't know whether or not I can trust him to tell me the truth. My gut is telling me not to trust him as far as I can throw him and that wouldn't be far at all.

"Yes," I answer him with what I know in my heart to be true. "Of course, he had no reason to hurt her."

"Did you know that she wanted to marry him when our divorce was final?" Johan laughs without humor.

"So? Everyone says that your marriage was over," I reply. "You were in here the other day with another woman and you expect me to believe that you're hurt here?"

"Oh, I am, dear one," he sneers. "Who do you think knocked up his old partner?"

"Luc?" I ask and an evil smile spreads across his face. It makes me feel sick to my stomach. He baited me, plain and simple and I hate that I fell for it.

"One in the same," he answers.

"I don't believe you." And I don't. Luc is a good man, a man whore, but a good man. He wouldn't be hooking up with anything that moves if he had a baby mama back home in the Midwest. Would he? Gah! I hate that Johan has made me so confused.

"But you don't know for sure, do you?" he questions. He must see the indecision written all over my face. I hate that I am such an open book. What you see with me is exactly what you get. But in times like these, it's not great. I'm at a disadvantage and it is putting me in a precarious situation.

"Here's your drink, Miss," the bartender says as he places the glass of champagne in front of me. "And congratulations on the win."

"Thank you," I reply honestly.

"Another underserved win," Johan snarks.

"We worked very hard for that win," I say before I can stop myself.

"Murderers don't deserve to win," he says on a sniff.

"I think I should go now," I say quietly as I pick up my glass and start to back away from the bar.

"Sure . . ." he says as he shrugs his shoulder as if it's no skin off of his nose. I don't stop to question it, I just turn around and move as fast as my legs can carry me back to our table.

I pull my seat out and plop down just as Trent joins

Kane on stage and they begin to belt out *The House of the Rising Sun*. I down half my glass of champagne in one sip.

"Oh my God!" Shelby practically yells. "Was that the husband of the girl that got murdered?"

"Yes," I answer her.

"What did he say to you?" Her eyes are wide with girl tribe indignation and I'm not going to lie, it feels good to have a group of great friends to support me in anything and everything.

"Thank you," I say as the waitress sets our meals down on the table in front of us.

"You're welcome," she says as she turns to leave.

"What the hell is this shit?" Verna bites out and we all turn to look at her. She has a burger, at least that's what I'm assuming that is, on her plate under an entire jar of mayonnaise.

"I believe that is the burger with mayo you asked for," Shelby says as she blinks innocently at her grandmother.

"Jesus Christ," she practically shouts. "I asked for mayo on my burger not a cum shot special!" The bit of my steak that I had just put in my mouth gets spit across the table and I choke on my laughter. These women never cease to surprise me.

"Now that's a cum shot," Daisy says.

"Don't they make cum shot shots?" Marla asks. "I think I want one."

"Now are you going to tell me what he said to you

or am I going to have to beat it out of you?" Shelby asks me once everyone is distracted again.

"He's just causing trouble." I shrug because there really is nothing that I can do about it. I learned a long time ago that I can't change other people, I can only change my reaction to them. So, I'm going to ignore him and go back to enjoying my night out with friends after a great day. But still . . . there's something that seems . . . off. I can't put my finger on it, but it's really bothering me. "There's something about him that gives me the creeps."

"Me too," she agrees and suddenly I'm sweating, and my head is spinning. I've had way too much champagne. "I think I need the restroom."

"Are you ok?" she asks me with genuine concern in her eyes.

"I'm suddenly not feeling so well," I tell her as I push my plate away from me on the table.

"That man would turn anyone's stomach," Verna chimes in.

I push my chair back from the table and start towards the restroom. I make it halfway across the room before I remember that I forgot my purse but that's alright. I just think that I need to splash some water on my face or the back of my neck. I smile a saucy drunk girl smile to Kane on my way. One that I hope sends sexy vibes to him while he sings on stage.

I make it all the way to the back hall when my feet stop working and I stagger towards bathroom door.

Son of Brian Orser's Silver Medal I must have drunk more champagne than I thought I did. What do they put in tequila in Korea anyways? Is it something more potent? I'm so lost in my thoughts that I do not realize that I am no longer alone. A fact that I would greatly regret in the coming moments.

"Are you alright?" The voice sends chills down my spine asks me and I know in my heart of hearts that I am not okay. I know that if I don't get away from them, I am going to die tonight. I was so stupid. I should have seen it coming. I should have known. You can't trust anyone.

"No," I answer honestly. I swallow back against the fear that's clogging my throat.

"That's alright," he purrs. "I'll help you."

"No," I say. "I don't want your help." But I can barely get the words out. Something is wrong, something is terribly wrong.

But it was too late, and everything goes black.

TWENTY

Stripped down and out of time and out of luck

My eyes flutter open and I have to blink several times to clear them. I move to raise my arm to rub at my blurry eyes but when it doesn't move I pull even harder.

It's then that I realize I am tied up.

Oh no.

Suddenly, the scene at the bar all comes back to me.

"Please don't do this," I beg Johan.

"I'm so sorry, but we have to," he explains to me.

"We?" I ask, and Natalie steps out of the bathroom and smiles at me and holding a small but wicked looking knife. It's then that I realize we are back in our room at the Olympic Village and I have no idea how I got here. "Natalie?"

"Hey, roomie," she calls out as she waves to me. "Fancy meeting you here."

"I see you've met my girlfriend," Johan says smugly and suddenly it all makes sense. Johan had a partner. That's how he could be in two places at once. I should have seen it sooner and now I'm going to die for my careless mistakes.

"I have," I answer. I know that if I have any chance at all of surviving that I have to keep them talking. I have to try and give Kane enough time to find me.

"Good," he says calmly. "We can get started then and don't have to worry about introductions and formalities."

I watch as Natalie sets the knife down on an end table just out of my reach. I look around I realize that I am completely naked. They must have removed my clothes while I was still unconscious.

"Why am I naked?" I ask them.

"It's really terribly tragic," Johan says as he ties more knots in the ropes that bind me. "You were having an affair with Saucier. He provided you with certain . . . tastes that your husband could not and would not provide you."

"I don't understand," I tell them honestly.

"Like Elin didn't understand Tiger," he says as he shrugs his shoulders. "Ambien helps embrace your wilder sexual nature. At least it does for me and it definitely did for Layla, so I can only assume that you would be the same."

"Don't worry," Natalie adds. "The effects will be totally worn off by now. Unfortunate because you aren't going to find any pleasure in this but neither did Layla."

"Kane will never believe it."

"Your new husband is a pretty jealous guy," Natalie says. "Am I right?"

Suddenly, that night that Natalie begged me to hang out with her came back to me. She seemed so lost and pathetic but she was really a wolf in sheep's clothing. I really need to stop trusting people. I feel so stupid. I did her hair and her makeup and told her all about my life. I spilled all of my secrets, my fears and desires to her thinking that she was a new friend. In reality she was plotting to kill me.

Natalie smiles like the cat that ate the canary which is an apt metaphor for her, really, when she realizes that I have finally figured out the whole of her treachery.

Kane will look guilty.

He's going to have a hell of a time proving that he didn't kill me and Luc in a fit of jealous rage. With seeds of their past conflicts and Kane's ex-wife thrown into the media spotlight, Kane is a dead man. He'll never see the United States or any sort of a free life again if these two have their way.

"It's not personal," Natalie says to me and I raise my eyebrow in question.

"Really?"

"It's not," she defends her position.

"You know what's funny?" I ask with a not at all funny laugh.

"What's that?"

"When we first got here, and I met you, I thought for the longest time that you were into Kane," I try and shrug my shoulder as best I can in the ropes and I move a little. Holy mother of Dorothy Hamill, I found a weak spot. Maybe if I can distract them, I can get out of this mess because Johan, that cocky killer, is total crap at sexual knot tying.

"Oh, I was," Natalie agrees with a chuckle.

"What?" I ask surprised

"WHAT?!" Johan shouts at the same time.

But Natalie doesn't care. She thinks he is her ticket out of here no matter what. I think I just found my distraction. If I can get these two to turn on each other maybe I can have the time that I need to wiggle out of all of this rope before they have a chance to kill me.

"Hey," she defends her answer. "He's hot and all the women he banged in our league back in the day are all coaches now. They swear he is a sex God with a cock to write home about."

I swallow back the vomit in my throat knowing that so many women have worshipped at Kane's altar makes me feel a little gross.

I kind of want to slap the hell out of him for being so free with his charms when I was just an awkward little girl at a skating rink, trying to hide from her psychotic step-mother and her dad who was uninterested in her life. But that seems ridiculous and also, immensely sad to think that that was the truth of my life. The rest of the truth is that through all of his faults, Kane has brought color into my world. And with him came a host of people that I couldn't live without. Kane, Shelby, Trent, Daisy, Alyssa, Verna, and Marla have all become the loving family that I never once thought I would experience.

But now I have, and I won't be fooled by this petty bullshit.

"Plus," Natalie continues not reading the drop in the temperature of the room. "Rich is rich. This one promised me a life in a country that doesn't extradite if I helped him. All while living off of pretty little Layla's life insurance. Did you know that there is such a thing as an Olympic clause?" she asks me.

"No," I answer honestly. "I had no idea."

But it totally makes sense. Johan had the chance to beat Luc and I for the Gold, it would have been close, but they could have done it if they skated well enough. But the chance to go home without his shrew of a wife and with a boatload of cash? I think I just found his motive to kill a wife that was going to leave him when they returned to their home nation.

"He gets four times the amount if she died before the Games and another three times that amount if she dies at the hands of the competition. Three more times!" she shouts incredulously.

"That's ridiculous," I say without thinking.

"That's what I said!" Natalie laughs. "But then he offered me bunch of cake to help him out and a one-way ticket to a South American country that doesn't extradite back to the U.S. That sounded pretty good to me, so I said sign me up!"

"So, it was you who drugged Luc before our practice?" I ask.

"Of course, I even killed Layla. Johan couldn't be anywhere near the rink because he already looked a little suspicious. So, he had to go sit in the tavern where we nabbed you tonight so that people could see him," she explains.

"And the French ice dancer that he was cozied up to?" I ask. "She was just another pawn?"

"What French ice dancer?" Natalie shouts.

"The one that my friends and I saw him pawing all over," I explain. "Truth be told it's rumored that she's quite flexible and willing to try just about anything." I wink at her.

"You bastard!" she screams before turning on him. "You said that I was the only one!"

"No, darling," I explain to her. "What you were was a fool who did all the dirty work by yourself and saved him from the death penalty in just about every country. I would bet he was never going to take you to South America because you are his plan B. If he can't make Kane look guilty, he's going to throw you right under the bus."

"That's not true. Johan is it?" she whirls on him.

"Of course, it's true," he says on a sigh. "And the girl is very bendy. I find that quite pleasing. And she lets me stick it in her butt."

"What is with all the interest in butt stuff," she asks.

"I mean . . ." I sort of shrug again.

"But the sex wasn't even that good!" Natalie shouts. "I'm sure Kane would have been better."

"Oh, he's fantastic," I tell her with a smile on my face.

"Maybe Kane and I can console each other," she says, and I don't like where this train of thought of hers is going so I start to frantically trying to wiggle out of the ropes while they turn on each other.

Natalie jumps on Johan and all of her experience playing ladies hockey has paid off because she is absolutely brutal at fighting. Poor Johan doesn't stand a chance.

I manage to get one arm free but the other won't come loose. No! I practically scream at the thought that I can't get out of here.

"I love you, Kane," I whisper into the universe with the knowledge that I will never see him again in this lifetime. I can only hope that he figures out what to do to prove his innocence and get back to the United States safely.

Just when I have completely given up hope, the room explodes.

The door to Natalie's and my room at the Olympic Village bursts inward and every single Dangerous Dame I have ever met runs in screaming a battle cry befitting a Braveheart warrior. Each one wielding a giant dildo over their heads and each one bigger than the one carried before them. Bless her heart, Marla has the biggest of them all. Kane, Trent, and Luc round out the crowd.

Johan and Natalie jump apart when they are startled by the screaming and the dildo waving.

I practically weep with joy to see them all. This is my family.

"What the fuck is this?" Luc roars.

"It was Johan the whole time," I explain to the crowd. "He wanted Layla's life insurance policy. They had some weird clauses that gave him a ton more money if she died before the Games and then even more if she was killed by a competitor."

"I knew it was you all along," Kane says to Johan. "I just had to figure out how to prove it."

"You were just in the wrong place at the wrong time," I tell Luc.

"And what about you?" he asks Natalie.

"I, like you, am just a victim here," she says as she starts to inch her way to the door.

"That's not true!" I shout. "She did all of his dirty work. She killed Layla and she drugged Luc with his Ambien."

"I really can't sleep without it," Johan explains.

"The jig is up now," Verna says.

"Ahh but now you are too late," he smiles as he pulls a gun from the back waistband of his pants and points it at me.

Darn it! I didn't see that one coming.

"How did you get a gun here?" Marla asks incredulously. "They wouldn't let me bring the eagle into the country."

"I don't play fairly," he smirks at the room at large. "Now, I'm going to need a private jet out of here and lots and lots of money."

Everything happens all at once.

Kane starts edging to put himself between Johan and me when he realizes that Johan isn't as close to me as he should be for someone who is supposed to be holding someone hostage.

The gun goes off and Kane dives in front of me as Johan screams—like a little girl, I might add—and drops to the floor blood spurting from his hand because faster than anyone could see, Trent picked up the knife where Natalie had left it on the end table and with alarming accuracy, hit Johan in the hand that held the gun making him drop it. Unfortunately, he pulled the trigger in the process.

Kane drops down to his knees and I see a patch of dark red growing on his shirt. He's been shot!

"Kane!" I scream.

"I'm okay," he says, and his voice sounds like he is anything but okay.

"Well, I'll just be going . . ." Natalie says quietly as she starts edging her way to the door.

"Get her, ladies!" Shelby cries in a fashion befitting a Civil War General and all the ladies hurtle their proffered phallics across the room, pummeling her until she falls in a heap of multi-colored plastic dicks.

"This would have been so much easier if they let me bring the eagle," Marla harrumphs.

"Nana," Trent admonishes but there is a loving twinkle in his eye that says he really feels like his grandmother could do no wrong.

"Police!" someone shouts from the doorway and we all turn. "Everyone freeze!"

I sigh. Here we go again.

"What in the bloody hell is going on in here?" the detective that Kane made friends with asks when he gets a good look around. I have to admit as I try and take it all in from his perspective, with Natalie unconscious in a heap of dildos, Johan rolling around on the ground with a knife in his hand, me naked and tied up on a chair, and the room full of two detectives from the United States and a sea of angry women, two of them over eighty years old. It's a sight to behold when you stop and think about it.

"I can explain that," Kane volunteers.

"Good," he says looking a little shell shocked. "I'm not going to lie, I can't wait for these Olympic Games to be over."

"Amen to that," I say from my place tied up in a chair.

"Oh shit!" Kane bites out before he begins to untie me.

When I'm free from all of the ropes his eyes narrow on the raw parts of my skin from where I tried to free myself. Kane looks as if he could he would strangle Johan who is now in police custody. Kane pulls his fleece jacket from his shoulders and wraps it around my body. He zips the sipper all the way up to my neck and the hem falls past my knees but I needed this. He holds me tight in his arms and winces at the pain that causes to his shoulder.

"Is it bad?" I ask him.

"It's just a graze," Trent says as he pokes at the wound. "Kane is just being a big pussy."

"Okay, asshole," Kane grounds out. "Next time, you be the one to get shot."

"How about next time no one gets shot," Shelby adds helpfully trying to diffuse the situation.

"Exactly," Marla wades into the fray. "Because next time I'm going to have the eagle with me."

"I'm really going to need you to give me that gun, Nana," Trent says with resignation.

"Not on your life, kiddo," she replies on a cackle and Verna joins in.

"How about there not be a next time," Kane suggests, and I can't help but feel like that solution holds a certain amount of merit.

"How did you make that shot anyways?" I ask Trent.

He just answers with a shrug of his shoulders and a one-word answer. "Ranger," as if that answers everything.

"Huh?" I ask.

"Trent was an Army Ranger," Kane whispers in my ear. "He's pretty great but don't tell him that. His ego is over inflated enough as it is."

"Ahh," I answer.

"I heard that you big hockey bastard," Trent says. "I saved your ass and I could still kick it too."

"I know, brother," Kane says as he holds out his hand to shake Trent's. "And I thank you for it."

EPILOGUE

Olympic Gold and fantastic surprises

Six weeks later . . .

Today is a really great day.

I walk in the front door of the massive Spanish style home that Kane and I purchased together after selling both of our condos. As it turns out, it wasn't hard at all to combine our lives because emotionally, we were both ready to do it. So combining bank accounts and buying a house was no big deal. While I will admit that I will miss certain parts of those homes—cough cough, the laundry rooms where Kane and I had our first dalliances before becoming a couple—I absolutely love this home. Mainly because it's ours together.

Also because it's in the same neighborhood that Trent lives in, so I get to see Shelby all the time. Shelby has become my closest friend over the last couple of weeks. She has really helped me overcome the lasting effects that I suffered from after my brush with death in Korea.

Which is why it bothers me so much that she's been left hanging out to dry while Kane and Trent work this new case. But that's neither here nor there.

I have every faith that she will pull through and if worse comes to worst, I'll be there to pull her out of it whether Kane likes it or not. And with the news I have to share with him tonight, he is decidedly not going to like it.

As it turned out Johan was right about somethings. Luc is the father of Miller's baby, but she was so afraid that he would leave her that she never told him. After our brush with death he went back to Chicago and confronted her. She had cried and apologized, and he promptly took her ass to the courthouse so she could make an honest man of him. Or at least that is how Kane reported it to me. They are now the proud parents of a bouncing baby girl. Her picture and a picture of the three of them are pinned to the refrigerator in the kitchen.

Kane and Luc also managed to put their past history aside once and for all and have become friends again. A fact that I could not be happier about. I had grown pretty fond of the ridiculous skater and I was glad to know that I was going to get to keep him.

They're even moving to San Diego in a month's time and I can't wait.

I was worried that I would have a hard time transition into professional life after being a competitor for so long but as it turns out, it's been amazing. Once word got out that I choreographed our programs for the Olympics, I have been receiving calls from all over the world. All manner of skaters want to come to San Diego so that I can choreograph their programs. It's amazing!

Not to mention, I am still coaching my little precision darlings and their season is just picking up. We have a national title to defend and we are ready to take it on. Not to mention that these girls are all so cute and funny and smart. They make me long for a little girl of my own that I can teach to skate. Or maybe even a little boy with Kane's blue eyes that will love hockey as much as his dad.

I drop my skate bag by the front door and slip my jacket off of my shoulders and hang it up in the closet by the front door.

I quickly kick off my chucks and run into the kitchen. I want everything to be perfect tonight when Kane comes home. I wash baking potatoes and wrap them in tinfoil after drizzling them with olive oil and salt and put them aside so that they are ready to go in the oven when it's done preheating.

I punch the buttons on the fancy oven that I absolutely love and get that heating up before turning to my steaks which I rub a steak seasoning that I mix myself on both sides before dropping them in a cast iron skillet full of melted butter to sear the sides. While that goes I run back over to the oven and toss the potatoes in before heading back to my restaurant quality stove and flip my steaks.

When I am sure that the steaks are browned to perfection, I tuck my hand into a potholder and open the oven to toss the whole thing in with the potatoes. I found this recipe on Pinterest and it has become an absolute favorite of ours. Who knew that I could be so domestic? Spoiler alert: it wasn't me but I'm actually enjoying it.

I head on over to the fridge and pull out my vegetables to chop for a salad and get to work washing and chopping them. I toss them in the big wooden bowl that I bought just for this house as I go.

The day we looked at this house, Kane and I went to lunch and window shopped after the viewing. I saw this bowl and decided then and there that I had to have it. Kane, who has not come to terms with my brush with death as I have, has decided to grant my every wish, something we need to talk about but not tonight. So, he bought it for me. The very next day our offer was accepted and thirty days later, my bowl, my man, and I took up residence.

I've just started on the cucumber when I hear the front door open and Kane come in. As he does every evening if I'm home already, he comes straight to me. Kane wraps himself around me from behind and nuzzles his face in my hair.

"I missed you today, Tink," he says in his gruff

voice.

"And I missed you," I respond as I set aside my knife and cucumber. "How was your day?"

"Good," he answers as I turn in his arms. "Frustrating but good."

"Are you making any headway to clear Shelby yet?" I ask, and he narrows his eyes on me.

"You, dear wife, are not supposed to know about that."

"And yet, I do," I say on a wink. "But that's not what I want to talk to you about."

He lets out a sigh. "We have to remain impartial," he warns me.

"I know, and I am," I promise my husband that I won't mess up his case as long as he does what he can to help my friend who seems to have gotten herself in quite a pickle.

"Good, now what did you want to talk to me about?"

"Come have a seat in the living room with me," I suggest.

"Now that makes me nervous," he says. "What are you up to?"

"There is nothing to be nervous about," I lie because I'm basically shaking as I work up the nerve to tell him my news—our news.

Kane takes my hand in his and walks with me into the living room where we sit side by side on the sofa that sits in front of the large stone fireplace that practically sold us on this house. Over the fireplace Kane hung a huge black and white print of him hugging me after my Medal Ceremony. I'm wearing my blue competition dress and a huge smile on my face. We have our arms wrapped around each other, but it's Kane's face that says it all. He is looking at me with so much love and pride stamped all over his face for the whole world to see. I love this picture and I smile every time I see it.

On either side of the print, Kane framed and hung his Gold Medal on one side, and mine on the other. He looks up to the picture as we settle into the sofa with a wistful expression on his face before turning to me.

"That was a great fucking day," he says softly.

"It was," I agree.

"Now what is it that has you so nervous to tell me?" he asks, and I should have known that my husband, Kane Fucking Green, would see right through my veneer to the heart of me.

"This," I say as I hand him the little plastic stick with the pink cap.

"Is this for real?" he asks me in a soft voice as he stares at the tiny stick in his hands.

"Yeah," I answer. "Are you happy?"

"I was wrong, baby," Kane says to me and I feel a little worried but something about the look on his face tells me that everything is going to be just fine.

"You were?" I ask him.

"Yeah," he says letting a huge smile spread across

his face. "Today is a great fucking day. The best."

"The best," I whisper as I repeat his words. A smile stretches across my face and I am helpless to stop it. And while happy tears slip down my cheeks I can't help but think that I am finally getting my little slice of a happy life because I know now that with Kane by my side, we may have our ups and downs, and fights along the way, but I will always be happy because with Kane and now this new little addition, I can't be anything but happy.

He pulls me into his arms and strips me down. Kane lays me on the rug in front of the fireplace while he removes his own clothing before covering my body with his. And then while our dinner burns, he makes love to me in a room that holds both our past and our future with two Gold medals on the wall and two pink lines on the coffee table.

I think things might settle down after this while Kane and I settle into family life.

Famous last words, right?

THE END

DEAD AND BURIED

Trapped in the Closet

D o you ever feel like you're stuck in an R. Kelly song? Because I'm definitely feeling like I'm living one. You could almost say I'm trapped in one. But not the toot toot, beep beep fun of "Ignition" or the motivational "I Believe I Can Fly"-- I'm talking "Trapped in the Closet." All seventy-five parts. Because, you know, I am actually trapped in a closet. A utility closet to be specific.

I have no idea what happened. One minute, I'm walking up the stairs of the building my granny lives in, Peaceful Sunset Retirement Village, singing, ironically, "Ignition." I had just gotten to the good part, you know, the "hot and fresh out the kitchen" part—it's the part where I like to mime driving a car, the part after the toots when I pull down my arm like I'm honking the horn on a big rig. I'm right in the middle of my song and dance repertoire—when all of a sudden, I hear one of the doors to the stairwell open and close, which is normal since the nurses and caregivers use these halls to get around faster and not clog up the elevators that the seniors use. The next thing I know, something hits me over the head, and it's lights out. I never even saw the guy. Or gal. Who am I to discriminate?

Anyhoo, fast forward, however long that might be, and I find myself awake, with a killer headache. A headache a lot like the one I got when I fell out of my friend's parents' camper in the second grade. My friend who was also named Shelby. Weird, right? Anyway, we were playing after school at her house, and her mom found nothing wrong with our playing in one of those VW vans that were small campers with the part that pops up out of the roof for you to sleep in.

So there we were, playing with our Super Spy Barbies in the pop-up part, when she jumped down to get a clothing change for her doll. Shelby B., as our teachers in school called her to distinguish between us, was a lot bigger than me. I was the runt of the litter back then. When she went to pull herself back up, dress included, she grabbed the board I was sitting on, and I wasn't big enough to hold the board down, so Other Shelby pulled me and the board down on top of her. We landed in order: board, then me, then the dolls and their accoutrements. After that, I bounced off of her and out the open sliding door onto the sidewalk, face first.

Next thing I knew, I was coming to, and her mom was running down the driveway with the phone to her ear. A couple of minutes later, my mom and dad pulled up in my mom's old Jeep Cherokee, followed by a fire truck and an ambulance.

As it turned out, I had one hell of a concussion, which we found out while my dad was hanging out with all of the firemen and paramedics that he knew because they all played basketball together at the gym. I spent the night in the emergency room and the next week with the mother of all headaches, which is how I feel right now as I struggle to open my eyes and make them focus.

I look around and everything is blurry. I blink my eyes a couple of times to clear my vision. It helps a little. I take stock of what's around me—there are mops and brooms, shelves of lightbulbs and other various paraphernalia, cleaning supplies—when it dawns on me where I am, which is how I find myself trapped in a utility closet, à la R. Kelly.

I'm sitting on the floor on my butt with my back against some more shelves. My legs are straight out in front of me, and my ankles are tied together with a zip tie. Yippee! I groan out loud when I realize my hands are bound the same way behind my back.

I could lie down and wait for a psycho to come back and finish me off, but that's not how my daddy raised me. And if I did die because I was being a big baby, Granny would bring me back to life just to whoop my butt and kill me again. I wiggle around, trying to find anything I can break these zip ties on. I notice the door has hinges that look like little hooks, and I scoot over to try to hook the tie on my ankles to it. I wiggle and kick my legs and wiggle some more, all pretty thankful I keep my biweekly yoga date with my grandmother and her friends.

I hook the zip tie on the bottom door hinge and kick my feet by bending and straightening my knees. "Come on, come on," I chant under my breath as I rub the plastic against the sharp side of the door hinge. "Yes!" I shout as the tie breaks. I swing to my knees and push up to my feet. My legs shake. Impressive considering there's a polka band playing in my head and I kind of want to puke.

I lean my right shoulder against the shelves and squeeze my eyes tight, hoping to stop the room from spinning before I can find something to undo the tie at my wrists. My eyes pop open at the sudden quiet rattle of the door. I have to squint against the intrusion of the bright light that is immediately switched on. When I open them again, I am face-to-face with the vibrant jade eyes of one sexy Detective Trenton Foyle, San Diego PD.

"Jesus, Shelby, you scared the shit out of me!" he booms. I just roll my eyes, which I instantly regret, slamming them shut again.

"What?" I ask innocently.

"You just can't help yourself, can you?" he asks.

"I don't understand what you're talking about," I say coyly.

"You just have to stir up trouble, don't you?" he asks, shaking his head.

I don't care to answer, so I don't. It's not like I find myself trapped in a closet every day. Who am I kidding? I may not find trouble, but trouble always has a way of finding me. I'd like to say this is the last time, but why lie? My name is Shelby Whitmore, and I'm sort of a reporter for the San Diego Metro News and most definitely trapped in a closet.

PLAYLIST

You Gotta Be—Des'ree

Payphone—Maroon 5 featuring Wiz Khalifa

Blue Tacoma—Russell Dickerson

It Ain't My Fault—Brothers Osborne

Attention—Charlie Puth

Take It From Me—Jordan Davis

Marry Me—Bruno Mars

Break Up In the End—Cole Swindell

Africa—Toto

The House of the Rising Sun—the Animals

Youngblood—5 seconds of Summer

Here Tonight—Brett Young

ABOUT JENNIFER

Jennifer is the USA Today Bestselling Author of the *Claire Goodnite series* and the *Presidential Affair series*. She is a native of San Diego, California. She credits her love of books and reading to her mother and her knowledge that real heroes do exist to her dad.

Jennifer is a graduate of California State University San Marcos where she studied Criminology and Justice Studies. She is also a member of Alpha Xi Delta.

She currently lives in East Texas with her husband, Sean, and their three children along with an entire menagerie of lovable but sofa eating animals. She can often be found on the soccer or baseball fields, reading, or wondering what the hell her senior citizens have gotten up to now. Jennifer is convinced that if she puts her apple watch on one of the dogs, she might finally make her step goals.

She loves a great romance, an alpha hero, and lots and lots of laughter.

Stalk her...
Website: jenniferrebeccaauthor.com
Facebook: facebook.com/jenniferrebeccaauthor
Instagram: instagram.com/xojenniferrebecca
TikTok: tiktok.com/@xojenniferrebecca
BookBub: bookbub.com/authors/jennifer-rebecca

ALSO BY JENNIFER

Claire Goodnite
Tell Me a Story
Tuck Me in Tight
Say a Sweet Prayer
Kiss Me Goodnight

Liam Goodnite
Hush Little Baby
Don't Say a Word

A Presidential Affair
The Senator's Secret
Caught by the Chief of Staff
The Press Secretary's Passion
The Vice President's Mistress

Royal Secrets and Lies
King of Lies
Crown of Thorns
Save the Queen
Tarnished Reign (Free Prequel)

Accidental Hex
Birthday Hex

The Alaskan Wildflowers
Wildflower

Funerals and Obituaries
Dead and Buried
Dead and Gone
Dead and Deceived

Murder on Ice
Attack Zone
Layback

Southern Heartbeats
Stand
Whiskey Lullaby

Standalones
Trap
Dark Horse
Counterplay

Sunnyvale with Alyssa Kale
Ready to Run

For a complete list vist:
www.jenniferrebeccaauthor.com/all-books

ACKNOWLEDGEMENTS

Thank you, dear readers, for being so patient with me and waiting forever until I could come back and finish both Shelby and Sophie's series. I hope it was worth the wait.

Thank you to Alyssa Garcia and Stephanie Atienza for putting up with me when life kicked my ass. I still maintain that I have only blown a deadline TWICE, so there. But still thank you for your grace and kindness while I find my balance. I wouldn't be here without you both. And if it all went away tomorrow, I would still hold your friendships as the precious gifts they are for the rest of my life.

And now we wait for Squishy to wrap us all around his little fingers. Our family is growing and changing, and I can't wait to see it all. Alyssa and I are going to be the very best Fairy Godmothers ever.

Thank you to Golden Czermak and Quin Biddle for the amazing cover image and for letting Alyssa and I have our way with it to be the perfect Kane.

Thank you to my mom and dad for providing ample material to inspire the Dames and their families for years to come and for being so excited when something ridiculous makes it into a book.

And lastly, thank you to my husband, Sean, who so bravely inspires comedic material with his unique outlook on life. Life with you is always and adventure and I am so blessed to be on the journey with you.

Your laugh is still one of my most favorite things in the entire universe. And thank you for sharing your Magikarp story with the world. But did you even splash, Bro? And through it all, you know that there was never anyone but you. Thank you for loving me the way that you do. For loving us all in a way that inspires love notes in romace novels.

Always and forever. To the moon and back

www.ingramcontent.com/pod-product-compliance
Lightning Source LLC
Chambersburg PA
CBHW072349020726
47506CB00004B/1063

* 9 7 8 1 7 3 2 0 7 4 7 8 1 *